Seed of Light

Edmund Cooper

In my end is my beginning . . .

CORONET BOOKS
Hodder and Stoughton

First published in 1959 by Ballantine Books Inc.,
New York

Coronet Edition 1977

The characters and situations in this book are entirely imaginary and bear no relation to any real person or actual happening

Printed and bound in Great Britain for
Hodder and Stoughton Paperbacks,
a division of Hodder and Stoughton Ltd.,
Mill Road, Dunton Green, Sevenoaks, Kent
(Editorial Office: 47 Bedford Square,
London, WC1 3DP) by
William Collins Sons & Co. Ltd.,
Glasgow

ISBN 0 340 21990 4

PREFACE

This novel, my second, was written in 1958 and first published in 1959. It received good notices, which encouraged me greatly. It was also published with considerable success in the U.S.A., West Germany, Italy and Japan.

The 1950's were dominated by two factors – the Cold War and the development of the hydrogen bomb.

In 1956, Russian tanks rumbled into Hungary to quell that country's brave bid for democratic freedom. The Hungarians appealed to the West for help. Their call was unheeded. Though the gentlemen in the Pentagon were breathing hard, the Eisenhower regime did not want a nuclear confrontation.

So the tanks won, and Hungary was 'pacified' – just as, much later, Czechoslovakia was similarly 'pacified'.

Seed of Light was written at a time when the Aldermaston marches were at their zenith, when a great many intelligent and well-meaning people saw fit to demonstrate their abhorrence of nuclear weapons. It seemed ludicrous that a small, vulnerable off-shore European island should presume to be a nuclear power.

Britain had already lost its imperial role. Two major wars in twenty-five years had seen to that. Two generations of young men had been used to fertilize 'some foreign field'. Jingoism was dead; but strangely, not too many Britons seemed to notice. The myth persisted – superbly enshrined in the Last Night of the Proms – *Rule Britannia, Land of Hope and Glory*, etc.

Now, in the mid 1970's, when Britain is economically and militarily at a low ebb, our pretensions as an effective nuclear power seem even more absurd.

Twenty years ago, at this time of writing, the West chose to avoid a nuclear confrontation over Hungary. Several years later, when a consignment of nuclear warheads was routed for Cuba, President Kennedy accepted the challenge; and that time, Russia backed down.

The Aldermaston fervour has waned. We all know that nuclear war is madness – the film *Dr. Strangelove* made the point admirably – and we have learned to live with the threat. We rely heavily on fail-safe systems and a modicum of international sanity.

But what would happen if, say, some extremist groups in the

Middle East or Central Africa managed to get hold of a few nuclear missiles? Would the conflict escalate?

The very existence of nuclear strike forces is, itself, a symptom of madness.

At the time of writing, NATO has a strike force of about 7000 nuclear warheads. Over 100,000 U.S. Servicemen have access to them. A recent Congressional Enquiry established that, in 1972 alone, more than 3000 of their key personnel were dismissed from service because of alcoholism, the use of drugs and/or mental instability.

Fail Safe? How can you guarantee fail-safe systems in the light of such facts?

The Russian capability is not accurately known. But the balance of terror is probably comparable.

In short, there are enough nuclear weapons, together with the missiles to deliver them, to destroy civilization completely.

What the situation will be like in a few years, when so-called Third World countries develop sufficient technology to produce their own nuclear weapons, I shudder to think.

Am I trying to frighten you?

Yes.

It is my task as a novelist to entertain. It is my duty as a human being to point out that, within the last quarter of a century, mankind itself has become an endangered species.

The first part of *Seed of Light* may have, I hope, at least a certain period charm; but I am convinced that the theme of the entire novel is even more relevant now than when it was written.

Edmund Cooper
February 1977

Part One

In the neighborhood lived a very famous dervish, who passed for the best philosopher in Turkey; him they went to consult: Pangloss, who was their spokesman, addressed him thus:

"Master, we come to entreat you to tell us why so strange an animal as man has been formed."

"Why do you trouble your head about it?" said the dervish. "Is it any business of yours?"

"But, my Reverend Father," said Candide, "there is a horrible deal of evil on the earth."

"What signifies it," said the dervish, "whether there is evil or good? When his Highness sends a ship to Egypt, does he trouble his head whether the rats in the vessel are at their ease or not?"

VOLTAIRE: Candide

Perhaps you think me mad, gentlemen? Well, if so, I plead guilty; I quite agree with you. Man is essentially a constructive animal—an animal for ever destined to strive towards a goal, and to apply himself to the pursuit of engineering, in the shape of ceaseless attempts to build a road which shall lead him to an unknown destination . . . Man loves to construct and to lay out roads—of that there can be no question; but why does he also love so passionately to bring about general ruin and chaos? Answer me that.

DOSTOEVSKY: Letters from the Underworld

BITTER HARVEST

Proem

Once, perhaps, Neanderthal Man felt like a conqueror. Was he not the Upright Animal—a weapon-maker, a tool-maker, an organizer of society? And with his weapons, his tools and his capacity for organization, could he not attack and overcome other individually more powerful animals?

Given enough time, his numbers would have increased and his skills developed sufficiently to make him Lord of the Forests; perhaps, ultimately, Lord of the Earth.

But he was not given enough time. He was already obsolete. For strangers came from the south and from the east. They, too, were upright animals—weapon-makers, tool-makers, organizers of society.

They came drifting into the world of Neanderthal Man in twos and threes, in families and tribes. And they brought with them weapons that were sharper, tools that were more functional, a society that was more tightly organized. They brought with them greater intelligence. They brought a death sentence.

They dispossessed the Neanderthals of their caves and their hunting-grounds, their food and even their children. For the newcomers were ruthless; and they fought a war of extermination.

So, after enduring for thousands of years, Neanderthal Man—the elite of European animal life—disappeared in a matter of generations. The conqueror had fallen before a greater conqueror. And the world was reserved for the exclusive domination of *homo sapiens* . . .

The history of Man is a history of conquest: the conquest of hunger and superstition, disease and ignorance. Beginning as a nomadic hunter, a seeker of berries and nuts and roots and small game, Man was not content with a simple destiny.

In the conquest of hunger, he learned how to make weapons that would kill at a distance; how to construct ingenious, self-operating traps. And eventually, he learned how to return the seeds of the wild wheat to the earth and thus safeguard himself against future hunger; how to domesticate and breed animals whose sole function was to serve, in living and dying, the needs of Man the master.

Families united into tribes, and tribes into nations. Cities and civilizations came into being—monuments to the abilities of Man as an organizer, Man as a builder, Man as an artist-scientist-priest. Man as a conqueror . . .

Records were made, sicknesses were cured, laws were formulated, empires were conceived, oceans and continents were crossed. Machines that were driven by wind and water gave way to machines that were driven by steam.

Intoxicated by his own genius, Man rushed headlong into the age of the powered machines. Coal and oil extended his conquests of land and sea and air. Electricity made a wishful daydream of remote and instantaneous communication into a commonplace reality . . .

But no conquest is absolute. What of the conquest of hunger if one man or one nation starves? What of the conquest of superstition if it is replaced by rigid orthodoxy? What of the conquest of power if Man wastes his surplus energy in destruction?

Man, the conqueror, ignored the problems posed by his triumphs. Instead, his pride sought new challenges.

Even before the old knowledge was integrated, before the old machines had been given a chance to fulfil their purpose, Man's curiosity, his intellectual arrogance, his insatiable desire for power drove him to reproduce the fantastic energies of the sun and lift his covetous eyes towards the stars.

In the beginning, Man was a hunter and a warrior. His nature had not changed. Even as he hunted down the secrets of the fierce energies of the sun, even as he used them to create new and terrible weapons, even as he dreamed of harnessing them to extend his conquest to the stars, all his triumphs were overshadowed by one lasting defeat.

He had survived every natural hazard of existence. He had triumphed over hunger, climate and disease. He had accepted every challenge the planet had to offer. And he had conquered everything—except himself.

Neanderthal Man had gone down before a superior enemy.

But, with the power at his command, Modern Man had no superior enemy—except himself.

There remained, therefore, only one basic threat to his ancient desire for racial immortality.

It was a threat that, until the atomic age, he had never seriously considered.

It was racial suicide.

Chapter One

The World

It was a fine June evening, and a pall of heat hung over the city like a sad benediction. The faint nostalgia of summer crept along dusty streets and half-deserted squares, feeling its way gently as a blind man towards the city's heart.

The man at the window stared out through a turquoise patch of sky between the hazy defiance of St. Paul's and the sharper outline of the Old Bailey. Those venerable landmarks still stood, quietly enduring: but even they had begun to wear the bright ephemeral glory of the doomed.

However, Sir Charles Craig was not at that moment engaged in his frequent and bitter pastime of counting the few architectural survivors of an atomic war. His grey, tired eyes were focussed upon some non-physical horizon, some elusive dimension where the past and the future were one and indivisible, and where the present was an abstraction without meaning. He was seeking an answer that he already knew—seeking it in the forlorn hope that history might be wrong; that some latter-day miracle might even yet fasten on to the heart of civilized man; and that London, as a fact and a symbol, might still be saved.

But there would be no miracle, for the future belonged to the past and the past could not be changed. For a hundred thousand years man had roamed heedlessly in his own condemned playground, fashioning club, axe, arrow, sword, cannon and bomb; tirelessly giving battle to the enemy that could never be defeated, the enemy within. And now, because of this, Pittsburgh, Detroit, Birmingham, Sheffield, Hamburg, Marseilles, Kharkov and Leningrad were no more: London, Paris and all the cities in the world were dying.

It was not pleasant to watch a civilization die; nor was it reasonable to carry on as if it would never happen.

As he gazed with unseeing eyes through the deepening patch of sky, Sir Charles wondered how he could hope to raise any confidence in a project which he himself regarded as already destined to fail. At best, this latest achievement was a shabby emulation of what had already been accomplished years ago—before atomic war wrought havoc with the economies of the great nations. It was a project that had virtually crippled the resources of the Commonwealth. And, at best, it would delay Armageddon until the eastern economy and the eastern scientists produced their inevitable answer. Unless . . . unless a miracle happened. A miracle of faith and understanding. A miracle of acceptance.

But while Sir Charles was prepared to work for a miracle, he could not bring himself to believe in it. Miracles were obsolete. They had gone out of fashion nearly two thousand years ago.

As he contemplated the latest synthetic star to be flung up into the heavens, Sir Charles remembered once more that first giant mushroom which, decades ago, had towered with sudden deathly beauty over a city called Hiroshima. Since then its terrible spores had blown about a helpless, fear-ridden world, swallowing city after city until those who remained intellectually alive knew that the end was in sight.

Sir Charles Craig, Prime Minister of what was still optimistically termed the United Kingdom, shrugged his shoulders and wished that he had never been born . . .

There was a movement in the room behind him. That would be Lord Drayton, his scientific adviser—the incomprehensible Drayton, whose mere presence was sufficient to make the Prime Minister believe that he was only a neurotic old pessimist, viewing the world with the jaundiced attitude of one who is too much alone.

Sir Charles gave a barely perceptible sigh, and turned his attention back to the room. Lord Drayton met him with a cheery smile.

"Ninety seconds to go, Charles. You ought to settle yourself in front of the stereo-camera and look a bit more confident . . . Is your chair still on the chalk-mark? There, that's better. You are supposed to be giving a message of hope, not a funeral oration."

"That," said Sir Charles, permitting himself a thin smile, "is a debatable point."

However, with a facility born of much experience, his

features began to register an expression of confidence—the discreet mask of the statesman.

Presently, the red light flickered. Sir Charles fingered his typescript nervously and cleared his throat.

"You know what *they* will be saying," whispered Drayton with a grin. "Twinkle, twinkle, little star. How I wonder what you are!"

An appreciative gleam came into the Prime Minister's eyes; and at that moment, his three-dimensional image came to life on ten million stereo-screens.

The man and the girl walked hand in hand along the edge of the fen. They watched the sun sinking low over fields of corn and sugar beet, over tumbledown thatched cottages and a ruined windmill. The air was heavy with all the scents of summer; heavy, too, with a dreamlike unreality. It was as if the whole scene was a backcloth which, presently, would be lifted when the lights died and the audience went home.

There was no visible indication that a landscape which had endured for centuries was nearing its end; but the signs were there for those who wished to read them. Over the hill behind the windmill was a large crater, a dustbowl, hundreds of yards in diameter. Once it had been an airfield runway; and before that, good farming land. Eleven miles to the east was another crater, a dead town, surrounded now by a pathetic fringe of prefabricated houses, shops and offices—more dead than ever with its thin halo of glass and concrete, its perimeter of insistent life.

Michael Spenser looked at his companion and wondered why she chose to isolate herself in this drowsy corner of East Anglia; why she should waste herself upon the routine activities of country life when there was so much to be seen, so much to be done, and so little time left? Then he looked again at the placid landscape and suddenly had the odd thought that she was no longer concerned with reality but with the preservation of this, her private dream.

She was twenty-three—seven years younger than himself. It was strange that Professor Bollinden's daughter should live here in an almost medieval simplicity while her father pushed the frontiers of science out into space once more.

But Mary Bollinden, as Michael had quickly learned, was a person who knew her own mind. She had inherited her father's characteristic determination, his ability to follow the course he had set himself with little or no compromise.

"People still get married, you know," said Michael, tentatively reopening an argument in which he had already been checkmated. "There have been wars before, and there will be wars again. History itself is one long blasted crisis. But the human race has survived it so far."

She gave him a quick smile, poised between affection and mockery.

"So far!" echoed Mary. "We have been incredibly silly and incredibly lucky . . . But it's not that. You know the real reason, don't you?"

"Like hell I do!" he expostulated. "There is no real reason. You're either in love so that you want to spend the rest of your lives together, or you're not. I think we're in love. What do you think?"

"That your terms of reference are wrong."

"Stop talking like your father."

She laughed. "You are a scientist, too. You should appreciate the objective approach . . . How long have we known each other?"

Michael gave her a glance of accusation. "Three years."

"Yet we have spent less than three months together."

"Is it measurable in time?"

"No, but it would have to be—if we were married."

"I haven't the slightest idea what you are getting at."

"Don't be angry, Michael, not on the last night . . . I'm only trying to say that you and I live in separate worlds. You are only really happy when you are in the desert, working on the project. I'm only happy here in England, living in what's left of the countryside."

"Living in the past!"

But Mary Bollinden was not to be drawn. "Perhaps," she said quietly. "And perhaps it is not such a bad thing to live in the past . . . Would you like to settle down here in the country, Michael?"

"I would not."

"Then you'll understand why I don't want to come with you to the Australian desert."

"At least, something is being built there," he countered. "Here everything is dropping to bits. All England is in a state of senile decay."

"No, it's not dropping to bits," she retorted. "It's being blown to bits—by the latter-day empire builders."

"Your father, apparently, is one of them."

"I know," she said evenly. "So are you. And I'm sorry for you both."

Michael shrugged. "We seem to be getting nowhere," he said in a voice that was strangely tired. "I wish I could take you with me, Mary. I wish—oh, I wish the whole bloody world was in love; then we could all begin to build a single cosmopolitan city that would make Utopia seem like a nineteenth century slum-town."

Detecting the note of weariness, Mary Bollinden tried to infuse a little gaiety into her own voice. "No more ifs and buts," she said lightly. "Let's go and watch Sir Charles let the cat out of the bag; and then we'll drink a bottle of wine to the new star."

Michael made an effort to respond. "All right, we'll declare an armistice . . . Just for tonight, I'll turn into a superphysicist and take the mainspring out of time."

Mary looked up at the deepening eastern sky. "When shall we be able to see it?"

"In about an hour and a half—with luck."

Hand in hand they walked up a drive lined with apple trees, and entered the small Tudor cottage. Its interior was a hotch-potch of now valuable period furniture. The only incongruous piece was a wide stereo-screen.

Glancing at the clock, Mary Bollinden went across to the screen and touched a small stud.

The two caretakers sat in magnetized tubular chairs by a table that was bolted to the deck. Through the plastiglass port window, the dark cloudy sub-continent of India seemed to be whirling in a slow flat spin.

One thousand and seventy-five miles below, what appeared to be a vast moonlit relief map was in reality a land teeming with four hundred million people—four hundred million different dream-worlds coursing through the great terrestrial night.

The view had lost much of its novelty. During the last twenty-four hours, the caretakers had watched the sun rise and set a dozen times. They were beginning to be immune to wonder.

Dr. Otto Rehn stared at Kingsford, his companion, speculatively and raised his glass.

"Already, John, we are what you would call, I think, a star-turn—literally so. Presently, the limelight will intensify

. . . I wonder how many million pairs of eyes will be searching for our new star?"

Kingsford smiled absently. He was a much younger man than the grey-haired Austrian scientist. At that moment, his thoughts were centered upon personal things—his wife waiting patiently, anxiously, in a tiny room lost in the immense stretches of the Australian desert; the baby that would be born remote from civilization, at the center of a new civilization, in the growing world of Rocket City. Kingsford was restlessly enduring a seventy-two hour tour of duty in the deep and silent world of space. He was more homesick than those first Spanish seamen stranded on the bright beaches of Mexico.

"Stop worrying about her," added Dr. Rehn before his companion could speak. "There are six more months to wait. It is going to seem a long time. I insist on delivering the baby myself, and you may shoot me out of hand if there is the slightest complication."

Kingsford gave a short embarrassed laugh. "Thanks, Otto. In that case, you should take out a policy. We might produce a super-Einstein with two heads and a built-in slide rule . . . I'm sorry to be so—"

"So philoprogenitive?" suggested Dr. Rehn slyly.

The younger man was amused. "That's the final proof! You *must* have learned the language from a dictionary . . . Isn't it time the Prime Minister spoke his little piece?"

"Another twelve minutes," said Dr. Rehn.

Kingsford allowed his gaze to wander out through the window to the terrestrial merry-go-round whose northern rim seemed to be the misty reaches of Tibet.

"I wonder what the eastern reaction will be," he said slowly. "Officially, they haven't even noticed us yet . . . Do you think they'll take it sitting down, Otto?"

"Certainly not," said Dr. Rehn emphatically. "It is not their custom to take anything 'sitting down', as you so aptly describe it. Do you forget that, twenty years ago, Russia was the first nation to successfully launch men into space?"

"One atomic war ago," observed Kingsford.

"Exactly. One atomic war ago . . . You are, perhaps, too young to remember it very clearly, John. But before the great powers allowed the problem of German re-unification to drive them into a war which bankrupted them industrially, technologically and spiritually, the possibility of deep space exploration was very close indeed. Even in the early sixties,

Russia had a manned satellite in orbit. So had America. Then the German problem came up again, the military men took over—and bang!"

Kingsford suppressed a yawn. "At least, our recovery program appears to have been more efficient than theirs."

"Nonsense! Have you ever been to Russia?"

"No."

"Or to America?"

"No."

"Then you cannot possibly appreciate the extent of the devastation. The Commonwealth was very lucky. It fought mainly a defensive war; and so it did not invite the same punishment . . . But soon it will be as crowded up here as it was once before."

"And then?"

"And then, John, the balance of bargaining power—or threat-power—will be restored," answered Dr. Rehn with equanimity.

"What is your personal opinion?" asked Kingsford. "Do you think we have achieved anything by throwing up another scientific swing-boat, or do you think it is all a waste of time? I hate to think that we have merely triggered another weapons race . . . Surely there ought to be a theoretical limit to the amount of stress, the amount of suffering, that humanity can stand."

"There is," replied the Austrian quietly. "It is death. Not individual death but racial death—the end of all ambition, of all power, of all neuroses, psychoses and every other disease that is the product of so-called civilization."

"So we have wasted our time."

"I did not say that, John. Personally, I think the most we can hope is that we have—as you would say—bought a little more time."

"Time for what?" demanded Kingsford gloomily.

"Time for you and Romelle to have a little more happiness," said Dr Rehn. "Time for your baby to be born."

"Or time for it to die!"

"Perhaps . . . But you don't really think that, John . . . It is the nature of man to act negatively but to dream and hope positively. That is why time is so important. The human race needs more time to understand its own predicament. It may be that the fears imposed by each new threat are cumulative. Perhaps the stress will become so great that humanity will be forced into buying enough time to find out what is wrong."

Kingsford pointed through the plastiglass window to the vast, rotating stretches of Asia shimmering in moonlight. "To blazes with abstractions! What happens when they catch up with us?" he asked bitterly. "We have worn ourselves out on a project that might give us an extra six months—if we are lucky. Then checkmate!"

Dr. Rehn shook his head. "War has been man's most absorbing industry for a long time. There has been no checkmate. There has only ever been a stalemate—and then the pieces have been set up all over again. The only possible checkmate lies in the finality of racial suicide or planetary unification. Sooner or later, there must be one world or an empty world." He gazed abstractly through the window. "By the time they have caught up with us, we may have created another device for buying more time. That is the art of survival."

"I can't make out whether you are an idealist or a cynic," said Kingsford in bewilderment.

"My dear John, I am much older than you. I am old enough to be both. It is the privilege of one who, in his youth, was a pacifist; and in his middle-age, a military rocketeer."

"The trouble with me," said Kingsford suddenly, "is that I'm just an ordinary bloody fool. I can fiddle about with equations and problems of heat and stress; but the philosophical implications behind it all leave me in a complete fog. As a scientist, I'm not bad: as a human being, I think I must be a damned menace. Here we are, sitting on something that may be instrumental in wiping out the race, and all I can think about is whether Romelle is going to have a normal birth . . . I should have got the ethics of the thing sorted out long before I came to the desert."

Dr. Rehn smiled. "I congratulate you on being entirely normal," he said. "That is why you are able to find some happiness; and that is why your faith remains unformulated, but positive—no matter what you say."

Kingsford sighed. "I shall be glad when the relief crew comes up," he said. "The kind of solitude you get up here makes three days seem like three years."

"If a day is to be measured arbitrarily from dawn to dawn," observed Dr. Rehn, pouring himself another whisky, "our tour of duty lasts thirty-six days . . . Do you know, John,

I have seen more sunrises in the last twenty-four hours than I have seen in my entire life."

"There's another one due shortly," said Kingsford. "I think they seem even more wonderful when you're a thousand miles up."

"Intoxicating," agreed Dr. Rehn. "A little more of this and I shall be feeling positively godlike."

"I wonder what the effect will be on the permanent crews," murmured Kingsford, sipping his own whisky slowly.

"Paranoia," said Dr. Rehn, with a curious smile. "They will begin to think of the poor devils down below as mere insect parasites wallowing in the thin green mould of the belts of vegetation."

"And then?" asked Kingsford.

"And then," continued Dr. Rehn, "they will watch the sunrise one incredibly beautiful morning, and they will understand that civilization is a superfluous nightmare. They will feel a divine indignation, a divine impatience. Then they will toss out the cobalt bombs, the virus capsules, the ionization units and bring this human comedy, this insect play, to a swift dramatic close."

"My God!" exclaimed Kingsford. "You're serious! No wonder the Old Man calls you Mephistopheles."

The Austrian laughed delightedly. "If you have read your Marlowe, John, you will recall that Mephistopheles was pledged to serve Faustus for four and twenty years; but I have only been with Professor Bollinden for three—so there is ample time to outwit the Devil."

Kingsford grinned. "I wonder if the Old Man knows what he is up against. After all, Faustus didn't manage to bring it off. He had literally to go to hell."

Dr. Otto Rehn flung a dramatic hand towards the plastiglass window and the dim rotating continent below:

"Within the bowels of these elements,
Where we are tortured and remain for ever:
Hell hath no limits, nor is circumscribed
In one self place; for where we are is hell,
And where hell is, there must we ever be:
And, to conclude, when all the world dissolves,
And every creature shall be purified,
All places shall be hell that are not heaven."

Kingsford put down his glass and clapped with ironic enthusiasm. "A scientist in the legendary Redgrave-Olivier tradition! You should have gone on the stage, Otto."

Dr. Rehn bowed ceremoniously. "All the world's a stage—but no, I may not be able to stop."

"Did you really mean it—about the paranoia?" persisted Kingsford.

"I think," said Dr. Rehn, "that I am slightly drunk. And when I am drunk, I talk much rubbish. Keep me away from the whisky, John, or I shall be declaiming Shakespeare when we make routine contact with Rocket City . . . It is not, perhaps, a brilliant distinction to be one of the few men to be tipsy a thousand miles above the earth."

"Hell's bells!" said Kingsford. "It's twenty-one fifteen, Greenwich Time. We'd better see what Sir Charles has got to say."

Being unused to a synthetic field of one-third gravity, he edged his way cautiously to the stereo-screen.

It was fifteen five. The air-conditioner was working perfectly and the room was cool, but the atmosphere around the long, whitewood conference table seemed dry and heavy. Every now and then, someone poured a glass of iced water, or lit a fresh cigar or cigarette, silently resenting the tension, the conference and the man in the light fawn suit at the end of the table.

Normally, President Hudson possessed an equable personality. If he had any outstanding talent it was, perhaps, a flair for inducing brilliant individualists—who tend to resent authority on principle—to unite their efforts in productive teamwork. But the stress of recent events had left their mark on the President. His confidence in himself and in the results achieved on the project under discussion was shaken. Too much, he felt, depended upon him and upon the men who now sat waiting for him to speak. Too much responsibility. For, if he interpreted the facts correctly, not only the fate of America hung in the balance but also the fate of an entire civilization.

Under such circumstances, the liberal atmosphere which he normally encouraged at meetings of this kind seemed impossible. Since the project had now acquired a life-or-death urgency, it seemed ludicrous to have to waste time on tactful persuasion or elaborately disguised censure. Time was now the overriding factor; and there was no time left for irrelevancies. He knew it—and he hoped that the men facing him knew it, that they would accept and understand the inevitable sacrifice of personal considerations in the name of speed.

"I presume, gentlemen," began the President with deceptive mildness, "that you have been able to give a little thought to recent events. For the past five years, we *assumed* we had a clear lead. And while we were busy congratulating ourselves on that happy fiction, the Commonwealth people were quietly achieving the impossible . . . What do you think they are going to do about it in Europe? And—even more important—what do you think they are going to do about it in Asia?"

He tapped the table emphatically. "Commonwealth has licked us on the stretch! Now some of you will have to explain how this happened, and why it happened. And I hope there are some really solid reasons!"

The men shuffled uncomfortably and stared at their blotters, their glasses of iced water, their cigars. Nobody spoke, and the silence became intolerable.

"Suppose we hear from Mr. Spartzheimer first!" snapped the President.

A dried-up, round-shouldered little man jerked suddenly as if he were a marionette galvanized into life at the sharp tug of unseen strings.

"Well, Mr. Spartzheimer," continued the President grimly, "as director of M.R.P., you might care to give us the picture on this timing error."

"Mr. President, gentlemen," began Spartzheimer with a nervous smile, "as you know, according to our preliminary schedule, we might have put the first one up six weeks ago. Of course, you all know that we are not primarily interested in the two-hour orbit; and, to that extent, there was no reason why we should consider ourselves to be in a race against Commonwealth."

"Kindly come to the point, sir," interrupted the President quietly.

"The point is, Mr. President," said Spartzheimer with some apprehension, "that the alloy we have to use will not stand the sub-strato acceleration stress relevant to the ninety-minute target . . . We need a tougher skin."

"That's fine," said President Hudson. There was a flicker of grim amusement in his eyes. "Just fine . . . Gentlemen, we need a tougher skin. Mr. Spartzheimer says so."

"The skin is all right," protested a younger man three places away from Spartzheimer. "We proved that alloy at a far higher weight/temperature ratio than you need for the ninety-minute project. Our reaction data shows that you could have pushed it up to a third stage velocity of thirty thousand, and the skin still wouldn't have gone soft."

The President glanced along the table. "I did not intend to call for your comment yet, Mr. Reynolds . . . We shall get around to you presently. And presently, also, we shall discuss those very interesting leaks in the Alloys Division."

Reynolds, a taut man in his early forties, turned red and sat down with parade-ground precision.

"Well, now," continued the President, "I have also been told that the t/n drive is not quite as efficient as we were led to believe. Perhaps we ought to hear what the Power Division has to say . . . Mr. Hemingwey, would you care to enlighten us?"

Hemingwey took his time standing up. "Mr. President, gentlemen," he began in a leisurely tone, "the Commonwealth people took a gamble on obsolete chemical propellants. We didn't think they could pull it off. But they did—and good luck to them."

There were sharp intakes of breath, and the President said drily: "I will see that your kind regards are communicated in the appropriate fashion, Mr. Hemingwey. Meanwhile—"

"Meanwhile, Mr. President," continued Hemingwey boldly, "we concentrated on the t/n drive, which is at least three times as efficient . . . Now, nobody can pretend that it was perfect or ready for operational work. There were plenty of bugs to be shaken out of it before we could expect top results. But political contingencies decreed that we should adopt a partial crash program . . . Even so, we might have made it but for one thing." He paused expectantly, and the President walked into the trap.

"I hope the excuse is a good one," remarked President Hudson.

"Yes, sir, it is . . . We lost Professor Galten. He was considered a bad security risk, so that was that! Since the t/n drive was Galten's own special baby, we have had a little difficulty finding an experienced wet nurse."

The President's frown deepened. "Professor Galten's political and social record, sir, render it inadvisable that he should have access to secret information. Our investigators have proved conclusively that he associated with proscribed organizations in the late 'fifties and early 'sixties. His suspension was made doubly necessary, Mr. Hemingwey, because of the frequency of sabotage in your Division. It is higher than anywhere else."

"Exactly," said Hemingwey unemotionally. "And I would inform you, Mr. President, that Galten's suspension has in no way diminished the sabotage. As for secret information, it is we, sir, who have been refused access! Professor Galten has forgotten more about the t/n drive than the rest of our boys will pick up in the next five years. That is why—"

"Thank you, Mr. Hemingwey. Please sit down."

"With pleasure, Mr. President."

Hemingwey resumed his chair amid shocked silence.

There was a hard gleam in the President's eyes. "Gentlemen," he said quietly, "I have no doubt that you can all provide excuses—of one kind or another. So can I, for my own failings . . . I'd be more inclined to listen to excuses if I didn't have to look up at the sky tonight and see something that is going to lose me a lot of sleep . . . We have lost the lead, gentlemen—but not for long. *You* are going to see to that! The latest deadline I can give you is the end of July. If anybody thinks we can't fulfil the ninety-minute project by then, he had better leave the project now." He gave each of them a penetrating glance.

Hemingwey stood up. "Good afternoon, Mr. President. Good afternoon, gentlemen. I sincerely regret having to admit it, but I do not think the t/n drive will be ready by the proposed deadline."

The President watched as Hemingwey calmly collected his papers and stuffed them into a brief case. His anger was mingled with a feeling of humiliation—and an awareness of the threat of more lost time. He knew that he needed Hemingwey, and knew that sooner or later he would have to be recalled.

"Kindly sit down, Mr. Hemingwey," said the President in a voice that was ominously calm. "Before you make your decision, I'd like you to share a little experience with the rest of us." He turned to a secretary, who had been trying to attract his attention for some time. "All right, Marshall, switch on the stereo . . . Gentlemen, we are about to hear an interesting policy statement. I hope you like it!"

And I beheld when he had opened the sixth seal, and, lo, there was a great earthquake; and the sun became black as sackcloth of hair, and the moon became as blood . . .

The sky was gray, welding the hard contours of the landscape into a uniform desolation of sky and land. There was yet no movement among the gray, barren stretches—nothing but a mute, gregarious cluster of steel and concrete ghosts. The fantastic geometry of half a dozen atomic cranes, dully brooding over a clutch of cubic eggs; the vast bowl of an amphitheater where, in a few hours, sleek totems would belch forth a language of green flame—all this, by day or night, was alive, purposeful. But now, at the edge of daybreak, it was vacant—mad with the fixed sanity of the dead.

The man looked up from his book and gazed through the window at that lifeless world. Presently, there would be a mechanical resurrection; but for the time being, there was such peace that a man was able to think.

The book in his hand was a collector's piece. It was several decades old, and there were now perhaps less than a dozen of that edition still in existence. Gazing through the window, Professor Bollinden idly recalled the day, long ago, when he had squandered the then princely sum of five guineas—a twenty-first birthday present from his mother—on that beautifully illustrated, hand-painted *Revelation of St. John the Divine.*

The days of fine printing, of books that lived and mirrored the love of the old-time craftsmen were gone forever. In a world of micro-film, stereo-screen, audiograph and transitape, books of any kind were becoming scarce. Printing, as a fine art, was dead.

Professor Bollinden fingered the rich binding, the tough hand-made paper, lovingly. He smiled at the thought that he, a 'space-scientist', a pioneer in the youngest science of them all, should feel such passion for what was non-functional, what was old and wonderful and lost.

The book was more than a personal souvenir: it was the symbol of a world that had been swallowed in the immensity of time—a world that was now as legendary as Atlantis, Carthage, Troy. A world that seemed now to belong to humanity's carefree childhood, to an age when only alchemists would dream of transmuting lead into gold . . . A dawn world . . .

Well, man had learned how to transmute lead into gold—if he wanted to. And much good it had done him . . .

But here was another dawn—another fragment of the total history dancing down the alleyways of time, like an old newspaper blown along a windy street . . .

Professor Bollinden shivered, and wrapped his dressing-gown closer. Here was he, a scientist at the summit of achievement—an old man with an old book at daybreak, waiting for the coffee to boil. He was, however, waiting for more than the coffee: he was waiting to discover the fate of a new, synthetic star. He wanted desperately to know whether it would become a star of mercy or of vengeance.

His eyes returned to the old familiar words set in a beautiful and obsolete Cloister Black. They seemed to glow on the page, to glow with the wisdom of men who had not yet been degraded into worshiping smooth metallic gods.

And the stars of heaven fell unto the earth, even as a fig tree casteth her untimely figs, when she is shaken of a mighty wind.

And the heaven departed as a scroll when it is rolled together; and every mountain and island were moved out of their places . . .

Would it come to that? Would humanity not be satisfied until the earth was reduced to a charred and crumbling wreck hurtling aimlessly round the sun; a lost celestial gravestone?

Professor Bollinden cursed himself for a thrice-damned fool. All his life, he had toiled patiently, methodically, *exclusively* at scientific problems. He never seemed to have had the time for human ones. Specialization was the thing! Leave all the ifs and buts to the philosophers, the politicians, the professional moralists. A scientist had no time to get bogged down in ethics . . . But who, then, had the time? A decision in London could be effected within minutes in Prague. A button pressed in Chicago could obliterate the problem of Stalingrad. Science was abolishing time. Soon there would be no time for thought at all . . . Or no time at all!

"I am an old man," said Professor Bollinden to the book in his hand. "I am an old man, and an utter fool . . . What is the use of speeding up the clock to catch a train to eternity? What is the use of hurtling through space when one has not yet learned to walk peacefully on the earth? What is the use of a machine that can outwit its master and destroy humanity? What is the use of a man who is not even half a man —who delegates logic to an electronic computer and ethics to a national anthem? God help me, I'm nothing but a clever imbecile, an idiot with a flair for mechanical toys!"

And the kings of the earth, and the great men, and the

rich men, and the chief captains, and the mighty men, and every bondman, and every free man, hid themselves in the dens and in the rocks of the mountains;

And said to the mountains and rocks, Fall on us, and hide us from the face of Him that sitteth on the throne, and from the wrath of the Lamb:

For the great day of His wrath is come: and who shall be able to stand?

The words seemed to be dancing, the book to be shimmering; but Professor Bollinden saw that it was only the strange, unaccountable tremor of his hands.

"I'm tired," he thought. "Dog-tired. It's the reaction, the sudden easing of the effort . . . I'll be all right in a day or two, when the realization that the job is over finally sinks in . . . But is it as easy as that? Or—or am I just beginning to learn what it is like to be human?"

He breathed deeply. The book fell from his trembling hands. But the professor did not notice. He stared through the window at the gray stillness; at the hard angular monsters that would presently grumble into a fierce mechanical parody of life; at the grim amphitheater where, presently, the continuous duel between man and his machines would be resumed.

There was no end to it; for the machines were incapable of realizing their simple victory, and humanity would never accept—or understand—its own defeat . . .

Professor Bollinden stared at the harsh surrealist world that had suddenly become his prison. With the sharp, dreamy awareness of a condemned man, he saw for the first time the true purpose of all the steel scaffolding in that bleak arena. And, gazing at it, he knew also why Judas chose the signal of a kiss . . .

A new star! Of hope or destruction? In the past, there had been too many other man-made stars to allow him the last, unassailable luxury of faith.

It was a cool morning, but there was sweat upon the professor's forehead. The world was still, but his hands were trembling. Presently, the sun would bathe the desert with living warmth; but he was afraid that this strange, insistent coldness would have already sunk too deep.

With a tremendous effort, Professor Bollinden sought to recover himself; sought to push down the inward darkness that was threatening to rise and swallow even the external dawn.

For a minute or two he stood still, his eyes vacant, willing himself to regain control.

Then suddenly he remembered his original purpose, the reason for entering this deceptive world of daybreak—the cause, perhaps, of all these human aberrations in the smooth scientific machine.

He glanced at his watch and, with somnambulistic calm, went across to the stereo switch.

Sir Charles Craig emptied all personal doubts, all private uncertainties from his mind and concentrated upon the effective delivery of his set speech. Lord Drayton, sitting out of range of the stereo-camera, experienced a strange momentary tension as the Prime Minister began.

"It is now my privilege and my duty," said Sir Charles, "to announce an important achievement by the Commonwealth of Nations. However, my message concerns not only the peoples of the Commonwealth, but also those of the entire world.

"I am, at this moment, awed by a terrible responsibility; for I must at the same time proclaim this achievement and make clear the only terms on which it may be faced with confidence by mankind.

"It is my duty to announce that a new manned satellite has been established in orbit over one thousand miles above the earth. It is my privilege to add that this accomplishment, which previous experience gives us ample reason to dread, may at the same time give us reason to rejoice.

"This citadel in space, circling the earth twelve times daily, is capable of delivering terrible engines of destruction to any point in the world. Controlled by one country or group of countries, it is—even more than its predecessors were—a most formidable weapon. Controlled by a truly international authority, it can be simply a celestial policeman—vigilant always for the general good.

"We of the Commonwealth of Nations have not established this citadel in space because we wish to dominate you of other countries. What we have done has been done in faith and desperation. We know—as everyone does—that this machine could be such an instrument of aggression as might precipitate war on a global scale once more. We also know that it *can* be an instrument of peace.

"If it remains exclusively controlled by the Commonwealth, whatever our intentions are, other nations would rightly regard this as a military or political challenge. Presently, other satellites would be established, each one increasing the tension and danger.

"As you all know, the old attempts at international co-operation—the League of Nations, the United Nations, the International Corps—failed tragically. And I doubt if there is any among us who has not suffered because of such failures.

"Perhaps, in trying to effect massive and general co-operation, despite the great variance in our political systems, we were hoping for too much, too soon. But, thank God, it is not in the nature of man to accept permanent failure—in any sphere. Is it too much, then, to hope that, where vast schemes of co-operation have failed, a simple and particular attempt at co-operation may succeed?

"In the name of the Commonwealth of Nations, I offer participation in the control of this satellite to the governments and peoples of the world. And in the name of humanity, I offer to mankind a way to ensure mutual peace. The satellite alone is not dangerous. As always, it is man who is a danger to himself.

"The appearance of a new star has long been recognized as a portent. This, too, is a portent. It may signify disaster or deliverance. But whatever happens, the responsibility must be collective. For this new star will react only as we react on the earth below.

"In conclusion, I would entreat statesmen and citizens everywhere to work against the common enemy. Once again, Science has provided a terrible challenge for humanity. But it has also given us the means to meet and vanquish the last, the greatest of all evils—distrust born of fear."

The red light died.

The Prime Minister sat quite still, and the mask of the statesman began to relax. In its place, there returned the gray, worn expression of a man prematurely aged, a man haunted by memories and premonitions.

Lord Drayton looked at the human being whose responsibility it had been to tell the world; who, by his indirect assault on world tensions, on prejudice of color, creed or race, seemed to be playing Russian roulette with fate.

He saw only an old man, lonely and afraid; a man broken on the rack of intolerable decisions.

Suddenly, without speaking, the Prime Minister got up and walked over to the window. His scientific adviser followed him.

"If that doesn't move them," said Drayton quietly, "nothing will . . . Don't take it so heavily, Charles. I have a hunch you may have pulled it off."

"Do you think so?" said Sir Charles Craig, gazing at the deepening sky over St. Paul's. "Do you really think so?"

His relentless, weary mind listed once more the cities that had already died; the cities that, even then, were dying.

"Hemingwey," said President Hudson, in what he hoped was a conciliatory tone, "we just have to have the ninety-minute project completed in six weeks . . . I'm being honest about this. I need you badly. If we don't throw this satellite up before the end of July, you can order roses for the western democracies. Because they will be finished."

The two men were sitting with their brandies in the President's library. President Hudson had decided that a private reconciliation would save much public loss of face. Besides, once the job was completed, it would be quite easy to reduce Hemingwey to life size.

"Personally, Mr. President," said Hemingwey, staring at his brandy, "not being a politician, I'm a little confused. Why this sudden urgency? The Commonwealth people have offered their satellite for international control. Now it seems to me, on that basis, it would be a darn good idea to have no more satellites at all . . . I'm old enough to remember last time."

"As you say, Hemingwey," retorted the President carefully, "you are a little confused. Now *I* can't advise *you* on how to perfect the t/n drive, and you can't be expected to advise me on foreign policy."

"No, sir, but—"

"Wait a minute, my friend, before you begin butting . . . I'll be frank with you, Hemingwey, and I hope that what I am going to say now will not be repeated." The President drew deeply on his cigar, knocked off the ash and regarded the glowing end speculatively. "We have information," he continued, "that the U.S.S.R. will be assembling their own satellite within ten weeks. I understand that, like Commonwealth, they are using the old chemical propellants. I trust I do not have to enlarge on the implications."

Hemingwey stared at him. "Do the Commonwealth people know this, sir?"

"They do," said the President. "Just to make sure it sank

in, I personally discussed the whole situation with Sir Charles Craig."

"What did he say?" asked Hemingwey intently.

The President pursed his lips, combining an expression of distaste with one of resignation. "Sir Charles Craig," he said slowly, "is an idealist. And, nowadays, an idealist in a position of power can be very dangerous. There is little room in the modern world for impractical dreamers. You know, Hemingwey, it may be that his speech on the stereo has set the scene for another global war . . . Commonwealth have put up their satellite. Well, all right! We think they mean well. If they would keep it as a diplomatic ace for dealing with the East, the situation would not be too bad. But they are throwing the darn thing away! Craig has offered it for world control. Now I ask you, Hemingwey, as a practical man, is that feasible at a time like this?"

"It's certainly a courageous gesture," said Hemingwey cautiously.

"Courageous!" snorted the President. "It's criminal lunacy! There are now going to be conferences—dozens of them; with the delegate from Indonesia telling everybody what to do, and the delegate from Israel telling 'em why they shouldn't do it. In short, a whole lot of time is going to be wasted—and that is just what certain countries want . . . I'll say this, Hemingwey, and I am not in the mood to exaggerate: when Commonwealth made that offer through Craig, they were—in effect—suggesting a mutual suicide pact for the western democracies!"

Hemingwey gazed at President Hudson, knowing that his statement contained a depressing element of reality. But at the same time, he could not help wondering what would happen if a few more of the world's leaders became infected by Craig's idealism. Unfortunately, it was only a wistful day-dream. It just couldn't happen.

The trouble with all governments was that they were composed of sensible, practical men—men who were not fools, but damned fools. Men who were so eminently sane that they preferred the inevitability of another global war to following up a quixotic gesture that held even the slenderest hope of peace.

Hemingwey sighed wearily. He knew what the answer was going to be; and knew that he, too, was just another damned fool.

"Well," said the President, after a silence of nearly half a minute, "what about it?"

Hemingwey shrugged. "There's the ghost of a chance, but only if we can have Galten back. Otherwise . . ."

President Hudson controlled himself. He had known from the beginning what Hemingwey's terms would be, but the confirmation in no way lessened his humiliation in having to climb down. "There is only one thing to do, then," he said heavily. "I will arrange for Professor Galten to be cleared. And I hope to heaven you know what you are doing!"

With a curious smile, Hemingwey finished his brandy.

Chapter Two

The Desert

The strato-rocket levelled off at a hundred thousand feet. It was travelling at mach four, but the illusion of stillness was profound and overwhelming. It was as if the rocket itself were the only motionless thing in the entire universe.

Up above, a thin blue radiance deepened towards the black empty canyons of space. Below, the hazy map-like contours of the Mediterranean countries drifted slowly along, playing hide and seek under low banks of cloud.

Michael Spenser leaned back on his seat and tried to recover the frame of mind necessary for the Western Desert. In a few more hours, he would be back at Base One, fifty miles north of Rocket City, immersed in the communication and transport problems posed by five thousand million cubic feet of underground accommodation, the highest point of which was a hundred and fifty feet below the surface of the desert.

The reason for such a vast undertaking had not been divulged officially; but Michael and his colleagues had formed their own conclusions. There was not only the refrigeration project, there were also vast dormitories, domestic offices, laboratories, workshops and several installations that were designated as 'surface-control chambers' and which were, in effect, complex electronic nerve-centers.

The general impression was one of a self-sufficient, subterranean fortress, capable of supporting its occupants for more than a year if necessary without surface contact. It seemed obvious that Base One was intended as a semi-permanent refuge in case things got hot in the atomic sense up above.

Sometimes, when he was working down below, Michael wondered if the idea of a semi-permanent refuge was all that the originators of Base One had in mind when they dreamed up that remarkable project. At times he had an odd conviction that similar projects were under way all over the world and that man, for so long the master of the planet, was slowly being driven underground by forces that he himself had released. Perhaps, ultimately, *homo sapiens* would evolve into a truly subterranean creature, having failed to adapt himself to the disconcerting freedoms and dangers of surface conditions . . . It would be strange if mankind, on the threshold of space-travel, was compelled to dig itself in. But there was also the grim thought that, probably, there would not be enough time for mankind to dig itself in satisfactorily. Time was at a high premium these days. There was never enough of it for so many things.

Michael leaned back on his seat and closed his eyes, shutting out the haze of daytime stars whose light probed the thin upper layers of the stratosphere. The sight was familiar, and the wonder ordinary—no more exciting than coral seabeds in the southern latitudes.

He tried to savor again the world he had recently left, the England of demolished cities and scarred countryside, the England whose legendary greatness had shrunk into the aura of a myth, incompatible with the paralysing sense of futility that seemed now to have fastened on to the country's heart.

Then his mind turned to Mary Bollinden. He pictured her with the moonlight pouring through the cottage window, illuminating the smooth tranquility of her relaxed features. He pictured her as he would always remember her, with a private serenity that remained untouched by the leaden fingers of the world. She had lain there on the old-fashioned wooden bed, not knowing that he was awake and engraving the moment in his memory, for she was lost in the unfathomable solitude of dreams.

Michael had been glad of that because, with an obscure fatalism, he had known it was the last time. And he had wanted to sit there until dawn, delighting in the quiet beauty of her body, recollecting the mobile pattern of their love.

It was strange, he thought bitterly, how she belonged to him and did not belong; how she had gladly given him such moments of love and yet refused to marry him and bear his children. In an earlier age, the situation might have been reversed. She might have been content with marriage and the creation of a family, yet unable to give herself to him as she had now done. It was as if human beings were forced by their own limitations to choose between love and responsibility . . .

Together, Michael and Mary seemed to hold the essence of the human predicament. Each could understand the other's attitude, and neither of them could give way. Mary's loyalty was to the old and valued things that were dying: Michael's lay with those that were yet to be born. Mary could not allow herself to bring more children into a world that was already unable to cope with its population: Michael, above all, needed faith in the future—in *some* kind of future . . . So they could love each other only to find themselves separated by instinctive loyalties. They could mirror in their own problems, and in a solution that was both impotent and sterile, the collective stress of civilization.

They had parted, and Michael knew that they would never see each other again. Mary would remain in East Anglia, would continue to give meaning to a landscape that was dying. Michael would return to Base One, a combined symbol of man's determination to destroy himself and yet survive . . .

As the strato-rocket streaked with silent purpose on towards the great rounded mass of India, Michael Spenser considered the problem of love and responsibility. Haunted by the image of a girl sleeping in the moonlight, mocked by the voices of children she would never bear, he wondered if there would ever come a time when human beings would understand that there must be no conflict between love and responsibility, since it is the greatest responsibility of all. One man, at least, had understood. But he had died nearly two thousand years ago.

With a conscious effort, Michael diverted his thoughts to more impersonal things. Less than twenty-four hours had passed since he had watched Sir Charles Craig deliver his speech over the stereo. But he had not yet considered the implications of the offer made by the British Prime Minister. Aware of a peculiar sense of detachment, he tried to estimate its effect on the Eastern Bloc, and therefore its consequent chances of success.

The helicopter ambled slowly past the great rocket launching site at an altitude of five hundred feet. The day was hot and cloudless; and the sun had turned the massive concrete structure into a smooth, blinding soup bowl. It seemed as if someone had dropped a giant silver cruet into the middle of the bowl, but Michael knew that it was the first stage of a ferry rocket which would presently blast up towards the two-hour orbit.

It was his first day of freedom since he had returned to Base One, and he was using it to pay a visit to Professor Bollinden at Rocket City. The fifty-mile journey by helicopter was a refreshing antidote to long claustrophobic hours spent underground; and Michael was feeling happier than he had felt for days.

As he passed the rocket launching site and headed towards the ever-growing cluster of buildings that was Rocket City, he wondered what frame of mind he would find the professor in now that the satellite was an accomplished fact. Would he be satisfied for a time, or would his restless energy compel him to press for permission to start work immediately on the moon project?

The last moon station—an American one—had been vaporized by an atomic missile during the war, and was immortalized only as an extremely small and recent crater among so many ancient giants. But before its destruction, it had accomplished much valuable research and had discovered that the moon was more than just a geological treasure-house since it afforded many rare metals and minerals that were now badly needed by an impoverished earth.

Michael knew that Professor Bollinden would never have had the chance of putting up his satellite but for its military possibilities, and knew also that military considerations held no appeal for the professor whatsoever. To him, they were only a convenient way of blackmailing the authorities for the money and resources he needed.

As he set the helicopter gently down, Michael wondered if Professor Bollinden would be able to use the same technique to persuade them to let him go on to the moon. He could easily imagine the arguments in favor of Commonwealth's establishing the next lunar base. But perhaps Sir Charles Craig's offer of international control would put a stop to all that. Perhaps, in a little while, it would no longer be necessary to use military arguments for the advancement of science. But perhaps, also, there would be no organized science left, for it was rumored that the East had construed Craig's offer as a thinly veiled threat. From their point of view, international control might carry implications of a bloodless democratic triumph; for an authoritarian state could not rest secure unless its subjects regarded it as the supreme expression of power.

Relinquishing such thoughts for those of a more personal nature, Michael made his way out of the helicopter parking ground and walked towards the professor's private apartments. He found Professor Bollinden sprawled in a deck chair on the sun balcony, reading an old scientific journal.

"Hello, Michael. It's good to see you again. Come out here with me and share the sunlight. I imagine you can't have enough time in the open. How are the dungeons progressing, by the way?"

Michael found another deck chair, opened it up and sat down. "Pretty well, as dungeons go. When I got back, there were ten million cubic feet ready for a good deep freeze. So any time you want cooling down, just give me a ring."

Professor Bollinden laughed. "Don't put ideas into my head. I could think of a number of eminent gentlemen I'd like to pop into cold storage."

"I have influence with the refrigeration section," said Michael lightly. "You deliver 'em and we'll freeze 'em . . . Anybody I know?"

Professor Bollinden gazed over the wall of the balcony towards the rocket launching site. "Practically all the world's politicians," he said. "That would be a nice beginning. And we could follow them up with every military scientist—present company not excepted. Then, having incarcerated the world's most dangerous people, we could lock the doors and lose the key . . . How's that for a program?" He looked quizzically at the young man by his side.

"It sounds frighteningly sane," said Michael. "When do we start?"

The professor sighed. "It would be very comforting to think that we could begin all over again, Michael . . . You know, since the satellite has been in orbit, I have had time on my hands for the first time in years. I have been thinking dangerous thoughts."

"What kind of dangerous thoughts?"

"The usual ones. The kind that make you wake up in the middle of the night and wonder why you were born. I have come to the conclusion that I am merely an educated imbecile—no, don't laugh, I'm deadly serious—and I think that verdict seems to hold good for most of us out here."

"Don't you think that's just a shade sour?" said Michael cautiously.

"Of course it's sour," retorted the professor. "I don't expect to be able to throw away a set of values I've had for a lifetime and still preserve a reasonable attitude . . . The trouble is, Michael, that I have only just learned what it is like to be human. A good scientist should never let himself do that if he wants to remain a good scientist."

"I don't think I follow," said Michael, afraid that he followed only too well.

"To specialize," continued the professor, "is to run the risk of losing one's humanity. In earlier centuries the danger was not too great, but nowadays it has multiplied itself tremendously until the odds are heavily against any specialist's remaining human. It is the price we have to pay for turning into a set of delicate calculating machines . . . And I'm afraid it's a price that is far too high."

"I think—" began Michael, but he was not allowed to finish.

"You think," interrupted the older man, "that I am suffering from overwork, perhaps. I am, and I know it. I have been suffering from overwork too long. If I hadn't been, I don't think I would have been such a fool as to plead, threaten and cajole them until they let me put the satellite up."

"If the satellite is the work of an imbecile," countered Michael, "then there is a serious shortage of imbeciles."

"You are still thinking of the satellite as a scientific instrument," said Professor Bollinden drily, "as, indeed, I used to do. But the satellite is the supreme expression of clever imbecility. And there are quite enough idiots engaged on similar projects in Russia and America, and elsewhere . . . You know, of course, what the conclusion will be? You know what it was last time."

"If history always repeated itself exactly," observed Michael, "there would never have been any progress. You will concede, I hope, that there has been a little progress during the last few thousand years?"

"Certainly," agreed the professor. "Stone clubs to hydrogen bombs; ju-ju to brainwashing; tabu to rigid orthodoxy; chivalry to total war; faith-healing to virus missiles; and murder to genocide. There has been a great deal of so-called progress. Perhaps we could have managed without it."

"But that is only one aspect!"

"Unfortunately," said Professor Bollinden, "it is the one that counts . . . Incidentally, you illustrate my thesis about specialization quite well. As a citizen, Michael, you are a good scientist: as a scientist, you are a dangerous citizen. The same holds good for me. That is why people like us can engage in so-called scientific projects without worrying our silly little minds about the consequences. But, of course, there never has been a purely scientific project; and that is where we come to grief."

"I know where this argument is going," said Michael. "It ends up in the old cul-de-sac: is the scientist who created the bomb as guilty as the man who dropped it?"

"Exactly. But that, as you say, is a cul-de-sac. It is also based upon false assumptions. The bomb in question is not a fortuitous product of science. If it is an efficient bomb, it is designed with a maxium weight/destruction ratio. In other words, it has been produced with the deliberate intention of damaging the species that created it. The man who conceived the bomb was already guilty of the greatest anti-social act as soon as he began to consider the problems of its development. And even if the bomb was never dropped at all, the man who contributed to its production would still remain a traitor to his species."

"But this argument can't be applied to the satellite," maintained Michael, "because you did not design it as, or hope it would become, a military weapon."

Professor Bollinden gave him a pitying smile. "Science teaches us all to be hypocrites, Michael. And we are trapped by the greatest hypocrisy of all when we persuade ourselves that any research is pure. The plain fact is that civilization started a gold-rush for power, and nobody can stop it or get out of it. The scientist wants power, the politician wants power, everybody wants power—the industrialists over the workers, and vice versa; the governments over the industrialists, and vice versa; the workers over the governments, and vice versa. Then come the great collective impulses for power: the big nations over the little ones; the white races over the colored; the communists over the democrats; and so on . . . And all the time we are looking for new weapons . . . You know how I persuaded them to let me put the satellite up, don't you? It was no good giving them a lot of high-falutin' nonsense. They wanted to know in plain terms whether—bearing in mind the materials we have to use these days—I could put one up with sufficient weapons, and the ability to deliver them with sufficient accuracy, to dominate the earth . . . The responsibility, Michael, was entirely mine. But I wanted to put that satellite up, and I didn't give two damns about anything else. And that was the greatest treason. If I'd stopped being scientific, and thought about the human results, I would never have gone ahead. After all, there are only two possible developments. The first is that whatever nation or group possesses the satellite will use it to dominate the earth and prevent any more being put up—if they can. The second possibility is that everybody will join in, and soon there will be another satellite war—only bigger and better, this time . . . Either way, the result is that man has a more efficient instrument with which to commit racial suicide."

"But what about international control?" asked Michael weakly. Hitherto, Professor Bollinden had seemed to be a man who was never at the mercy of his emotions. This was the first time Michael had seen the passion and indignation of the man break through the mask of the scientist.

"International bull-shooting!" exclaimed the professor. "The only things that are international are things like air, sunlight and death. All three are provided gratis, but man has seen fit to mass-produce the last."

"Somehow," said Michael, at a loss, "I never thought of you as a cynic. It seemed to me that there must be an overwhelming purpose—a *positive* purpose—behind your drive."

"I am not a cynic," retorted Professor Bollinden. "I am merely an unintelligent idealist whose ideals are suffering from senile decay. As for the overwhelming purpose, as you call it, that can neatly be defined in terms of the death-wish that infects us all . . . When I was a young man, Michael, about your age, I spent half my time dreaming up Utopias on a scientific basis. That was my first mistake. I should have realized that any paradise that man was likely to achieve would be in spite of science and not because of it."

"I think," said Michael, "that I could use a drink. It might help me to decide whether you are trying to pull my leg or break my nerve."

"Help yourself," said the professor, indicating a tray. "And pour me a large one while you're about it. During the last few days, I have developed a new respect for alcohol. If you drink enough of it, it stops your being scientific and gives you time to be human."

Michael noticed that one of the bottles of whisky was empty, but he said nothing. Professor Bollinden, normally an abstainer, seemed to be in a period of great stress. As he poured the drinks, Michael tried to convince himself that it was a nervous reaction to the tremendous effort of the last few weeks. But he knew that it would take something deeper than exhaustion to make such cracks in the scientist's intellectual armor. He had a feeling that there was a particular problem haunting the professor, of which the satellite was only an external symbol.

"Thank you, Michael," said Professor Bollinden, taking his glass. "I'm sorry to go up like a fireball as soon as I see you; but better you than some of the scientific cretins there are around here. They grow like weeds." He pointed across the balcony towards the launching site. "They are begotten of steel and concrete, acid and rocket motors. They leap out fully armed from slide-rules and test-tubes. And their only function is to worship at the shrine of the whining totem." He laughed harshly. "In short, they are the first successful robots of the age of disintegration."

"I drink to all our colleagues," announced Michael gravely. "Otto will be very interested to learn how he was born."

Professor Bollinden smiled. "Otto, like me, belongs to the Old Guard. We are the last of the Mohicans. I think he dislikes these clever boys from the technical colleges as much as I do."

"Talking of Otto," said Michael, deftly changing the conversational trend, "I hear he has done a tour of duty with Kingsford up in the satellite. I must get him to tell me what it feels like to hurtle round the world at sixteen thousand miles an hour."

"He says," remarked Professor Bollinden drily, "that he went up relatively normal, but that he came down with a dangerously ingrowing paranoia. I gather he was tempted to chuck out the cobalt bombs and give the planet a new start."

"What stopped him?" inquired Michael with a smile.

"They hadn't ferried up the reserve supply and the Stort-Mannheim radio fuses. According to Otto, he would only have had enough stuff to wipe out a small continent. So he decided to leave the job to the professionals . . . Good old Mephistopheles! He is so uninhibited about his secret impulses that I think he must be the only sane one among us."

Michael laughed. "I don't think I'm going to sleep very well if he goes up there again."

"In that case," said the professor with an odd smile, "you ought to book yourself a couple of restless nights at the end of this week, because he and I are going up to push through a few reaction tests before the damned military begin to interfere too much . . . Incidentally, have you heard that Sir Charles Craig and his faithful hound Drayton are paying us a visit?"

"No, I haven't . . . What is the reason? I don't suppose they are coming out just to enjoy the desert scenery or watch a three-stager shoot up to the orbit."

Professor Bollinden made a wry face. "They will be wearing black ties. I expect they have seen the writing on the wall. I used to have faith in Craig—of a kind—but I'm afraid he is ample proof that the way to hell is paved with good intentions. Drayton is another sort of fish altogether. He likes to pretend that nothing surprises him. As a matter of fact, it was Drayton who persuaded Sir Charles to let me put the thing up. And if I wanted to push on to the moon, it would be Drayton who would fix up the political side—on the understanding that our first task would be to fix up a lunar base for delivering missiles back to earth . . . A nice character, Lord Drayton. The perfect example of a military scientist—which is synonymous with homicidal maniac."

"I heard Craig's speech while I was staying with Mary," ventured Michael. "It *sounded* all right."

"Ah yes, Mary," said the professor. "I've been ranting so much I haven't even asked you about her. How is she, Michael? Is she happy?"

"I think she's happy," said Michael, and then he added ruefully: "She still won't marry me, and I don't know whether she's happy in spite of that or because of it. She has inherited your obstinacy."

"Plus her mother's common sense," observed Professor Bollinden with conviction. "I used to believe that her mother divorced me out of boredom, but I'm beginning to have second thoughts . . . What does Mary think about our activities?"

Michael gave a bitter laugh. "She calls us latter-day empire builders, and seems to regard all scientists with that cautious pity one usually reserves for mad dogs."

"Good for her!" said the professor. "She's more intelligent than you and I rolled together . . . Is she in love with you, Michael?"

He nodded. "That's what makes the situation so damned funny. She won't come out to the desert, and I won't chuck up my work at Base One."

"If I were you," said Professor Bollinden, "I wouldn't

think twice about it. I'd catch the next strato-rocket back to England . . . It has taken me forty years to discover what Mary instinctively knows. Why don't you go back and get her to teach you how to be sane—before it's too late?"

"Because," answered Michael in a flat voice. "it's already too late . . . That's what you have just been telling me, isn't it?"

The older man did not meet his gaze. "I want to know all about her cottage," he said softly. "The one in East Anglia. I have never had time to go there myself. Of course, she's sent me photographs and reams of description . . . But I'd like to hear all about it. Will it hurt much to tell me, Michael?"

"No more than it does when I think about it." Then he added lightly: "I wonder what you would have been like as a father-in-law?"

"Appalling," decided Professor Bollinden with a grin. "I am the greatest argument I know for not marrying her . . . But I would have liked to have grandchildren to spoil, all the same."

They stayed out on the balcony until sunset. talking about a world that seemed to be light-years away from Rocket City. And as they talked, they watched the preparations for the launching of another ferry rocket in the wide concrete basin.

Presently, it would rise in a sharp scream of flame, taking its cargo of men, instruments, supplies and lethal weapons up through the atmospheric veil to the hard uncompromising clarity of space.

Presently, that pin-point citadel, circling the world like a mechanical moth, would concentrate enough power to challenge the established order of life on the planet; to attack its own matrix; to purge, with clean blasts of solar heat, the fantastic arrogance of *homo sapiens*.

"So we have failed after all." said Professor Bollinden slowly. Sir Charles gave him a searching look. "That appears to be the general impression," he admitted. "The world doesn't seem to care for the idea of a celestial policeman—at least, not the kind we can supply."

The five men in the conference room stared at each other, their eyes asking the same silent question. Besides Sir Charles Craig, Lord Drayton and Professor Bollinden, there was Hervey-Walton, director of Base One, and Colonel Jensen,

Chief Security Officer for both Rocket City and the underground project.

"Of course," continued Sir Charles, "there is always the possibility of a more intelligent reaction at the next General Assembly. I think, however, that not even the most optimistic of us expects the Eastern Bloc to suffer a change of heart. They are attending the discussions merely as a delaying tactic. If they can avoid any decision for the next couple of months, they will be in a position to turn the whole thing into another weapons scramble."

"In which case," said Professor Bollinden, "we shall be back where we started—except that we now possess more efficient methods of racial extermination."

Then Hervey-Walton spoke. The director of Base One was a small, saturnine man with a perpetually worried expression. "Is there any possibility of going ahead on our own, Sir Charles?"

The Prime Minister shook his head. "I'm being frank with you people. I have to be, because the situation is too serious for prevarication. Naturally, that possibility will be discussed at the meeting of Commonwealth Ministers; but you can imagine what would happen if we said, in effect, to Russia: All right, if you don't want to co-operate, we'll do it ourselves . . . First, if such a policy were to produce any results, we should have to ensure that they could not put up a satellite—and that would mean offensive action. Second, they could neatly steal the initiative by demanding that the American program be also abandoned . . . And I am afraid, gentlemen, that America has virtually adopted the same attitude."

There was a brief silence. The director of Base One was about to make a further suggestion when he was forestalled by Lord Drayton.

"As a matter of fact," said the scientific adviser, "we have only ourselves to blame—both for the narrow time margin and for placing Russia in such a strong position. As Colonel Jensen is already aware, it has been established beyond any shadow of doubt that the security here at Rocket City is unsound. Information has filtered through which proves that at least one key scientist on the project is in contact with Soviet agents."

"Who?" demanded Professor Bollinden.

Colonel Jensen looked up from the pad on which he was doodling and spoke for the first time. "We don't know," he said bluntly. "I even suspected you at one stage, Professor."

Professor Bollinden began to laugh.

As the sun sank towards the western horizon, the contours of the desert began to soften. Michael looked back at the startlingly small group of huts, over a mile away, that was all to be seen of the vast installation of Base One. Below those huts was the tortuous maze of passageways and chambers—like a giant formicary—whose transformation into a self-sufficient refuge was nearing completion.

Ahead and all around were the empty stretches of desert, stony and inhospitable, relieved only by occasional scant green bushes and an odd stunted tree.

Michael was alone. It was his custom, after spending a day wrestling with transport and communication problems two hundred feet below the earth's surface, to take a stroll before sunset in the solitude of the desert. Often, when he was far enough away from the installations, he would relapse into a private game of pretending that he was the last man alive. He would imagine a world of dead cities, of desolate continents and restless ghosts—a huge, empty mansion gyrating dreamily under the impassive stars. A broken contract; a promise that was never fulfilled . . .

He could not understand why he should indulge in such a fantastic notion—except, perhaps, that it might be a sort of catharsis of private and professional frustrations. He would scarcely admit it; but in some way the fancy pleased him, inducing a bitter exultation, an ecstasy of loneliness in which he felt his identity peeling away until nothing mattered any more but the voice of the wind.

He walked on into the desert, unconscious of his surroundings or the direction he took, until it seemed as if Base One and the world it symbolized were nothing but a transient dream, a momentary pattern of movement on the fine web of time. He did not realize that the sun had gone down, or that the world was becoming dark—not until he heard the full, piercing whine that, in the Western Desert, meant only one thing. Automatically, he glanced south across the shadowy landscape. There, in the distance, a thin green tongue of flame seemed to hover above the horizon. Then slowly, majestically, it began to rise.

The rocket itself could not be seen; but as the green flame climbed and lengthened into a hazy filament, Michael knew that, ahead of it, was a smooth metallic pencil the size of an old-fashioned destroyer, accelerating at thousands of miles an hour in its upward leap into space.

And then, suddenly the rocket broke free of earth's shadow and surged clear into the hard sunlight. There, miraculously, it bloomed like a bright ascending star.

Michael watched, transfixed, and felt a quick pride that he should belong to a race capable of accepting the dark challenge of space. He gazed at the sunlit rocket until it was no more than a sharp, luminous point a thousand miles away in the two-hour orbit. Then he remembered its cargo, the payload of latent destruction being ferried up to an outpost that might have been a springboard for the stars, but wasn't. An outpost that humanity had turned into a loaded pistol, pointing at the great head of the world.

Pride evaporated as quickly as it had grown. He began to wonder why so many of the great achievements of humanity, begun in courage, should be perverted by fear. In an unfamiliar mood of despondency, of shame at his own unquestioning acceptance of the desert project, he turned round and made his way back to Base One.

Overhead, the desert sky revealed a fine dust of stars. But as he gazed at them, the disillusioned words of Professor Bollinden echoed in his ears.

"Well, Otto," said Professor Bollinden, "I don't think there is any excuse for either of us. We should have had more sense. It would have been better to have spent our declining years studying human psychology and social history."

It was after sunset, and the two men were relaxing in the professor's study. It had been a tiring day. Sir Charles Craig and Lord Drayton had inspected the laboratories, fuel plants, test pads, workshops, the assembly and recovery stations, and finally the launching site. Then Lord Drayton had presided over a full-scale conference on the intricate problems of logistics created by the satellite. Drayton, being a scientist himself, was not content with generalizations . . . A very tiring day.

Dr. Rehn poured himself another lager, and lit a cigarette. "He who expects little is rarely disappointed. Unlike you, Dennis, I had no great hopes for the satellite. After all, look what happened to the others . . . *Homo solus aut deus aut demon*. Well, man is always alone, and since he is rarely godlike, he is usually the very devil." He raised his glass. "I drink to human nature."

"Human nature," echoed the professor. "What is human nature?"

"The capacity to be idiotically intelligent and divinely stupid," answered Dr. Rehn.

"You have a Teutonic mania for aphorisms," said Bollinden with a smile. "However, it isn't a bad one. But since you are so fond of Latin, here is another tag for the collection: *homo sum, et nihil humani a me alienum puto.*"

"I am a man, and nothing human is alien to me . . . Is that it?"

"Exactly. In other words, my dear Otto, we can't pretend to be objective about the human race and regard it as a bunch of experimental guinea pigs. We have the same disease. You and I have displayed quite enough idiotic intelligence. It is time we produced some divine stupidity."

"In relation to the satellite?"

"In relation to the satellite."

Dr. Rehn lowered his gaze and appeared to contemplate his lager. "But after all, Dennis, the problem is really out of our hands. They wanted the satellite, and we provided it. The question of its use is one for the politicians and—God save us—the military."

"The question of its use is one for human beings," corrected the professor. "Especially the blasted fools who put it up. Don't you think it is time we stopped depositing scientific babies on political doorsteps?"

"As one blasted fool to another," said Dr. Rehn equably, "do you think the Commonwealth Council would be likely to take any notice of our suggestions—assuming, of course, that we have any?"

Professor Bollinden did not answer immediately. He seemed to give his whole attention to the filling and lighting of a very ancient pipe. At last, he said: "There is the theoretical possibility of independent action, Otto."

Dr. Rehn gazed at his companion, and chose his words carefully: "In another three days, there will be a military crew aboard the satellite . . . How would you define independent action?"

The professor bypassed the direct question. "In another few weeks—barring pestilence, warfare and an act of God—our Russian colleagues will provide their own answer to Commonwealth satellite. Followed closely, no doubt, by the Americans—assuming Galten has luck with his t/n drive . . . Not so long ago, everybody thought it would be years before any of the great powers could put up another satellite. But it appears that every country underestimated every other country's recovery program. We know what happened last time when there were several satellites up aloft—and they weren't very efficient ones. What do you think is going to happen this time?"

The Austrian smiled. "Bang!" he said. "Bang! Bang! Bang!"

"We agree on the prognosis, then," said the professor calmly.

"It is merely a question of time," remarked Dr. Rehn.

"Time is shrinking. What we need is some decisive action while there is still only one satellite."

"Certainly. But it will not come from Sir Charles Craig. So there remains—what?"

Professor Bollinden gazed at his colleague somberly. "An act of God," he said. "That is all we can hope for now."

Dr. Rehn was amused. "My dear Dennis, I have known you over three years and never suspected that you were religious."

The professor did not smile. "Why else should I sell my soul to the Devil dressed up as the great god Science?" he demanded. "Mephistopheles, you disappoint me. I would have credited you with more perception . . . All fanaticism springs from the religious impulse. I, being a typical product of the times, was content to accept the arguments of the Devil's Advocate on their face value . . . It has taken me a lifetime to realize that man himself is the most important act of God, and must therefore accept his own responsibility."

"Your metaphysics are loose, but interesting," observed Dr. Rehn drily. "However, I fail to see any relevance."

Professor Bollinden got up from his chair and walked over to the window, gazing with unseeing eyes out into the desert night. "Responsibility," he said quietly, "is the key. We have re-created this terrible problem for the world—and, once more, the world is unable to cope with it. Otto, we can't just disassociate ourselves. We must attempt a solution."

Dr. Rehn gazed at his companion thoughtfully. "Tomorrow," he said, "we go up for the last test in the reaction series. We shall have plenty of time to consider the problem in the appropriate locale. One has time to think when one is hurtling round the earth at sixteen thousand miles an hour. One feels strangely still . . ." He paused, then added suddenly: "You are not proposing to destroy the satellite, are you, Dennis? Because that would be no solution at all."

Professor Bollinden turned from the window. His eyes seemed unusually brilliant. "No," he said softly. "I am merely proposing to become an act of God."

"Mr. Spenser wanted on R.T.!" called out one of the men.

Michael made his way down the length of the chamber to the large packing case that did service as a portable telephone hut.

"Who is it?"

"Prime Minister," said the man laconically.

Michael grinned, and lifted the instrument.

"Mr. Michael Spenser?" enquired the voice.

"Speaking."

"Good. Sir Charles Craig here. How soon can you get to Rocket City, Mr. Spenser?"

"In about twenty minutes, Sir Charles," said Michael, recognizing the familiar voice with a shock.

"We shall expect you. I may say that we need your co-operation urgently. I—er—believe you are a close friend of Professor Bollinden?"

"The professor tolerates my company," said Michael cautiously, wondering what it was all about.

"Then you may be of considerable help," said Sir Charles. "I will put you in the picture when you get here . . . Time is important. Goodbye."

"Goodbye, Sir Charles. I'll leave immediately."

Michael replaced the receiver. His mind was besieged by too many questions.

Sir Charles Craig, Lord Drayton and Hervey-Walton, the director of Base One, were in the Communications Office at the launching site. On one of the walls was a panel of stereo-screens, and below this the tuning controls. At the other end of the long room was a small window, six inches thick. Through it could be seen the impressive shape of a three-stage rocket standing in readiness for firing point.

Hervey-Walton began to manipulate the stereo controls. He glanced at the time/movement chart on the wall. "The satellite will be in stereo range in about ten minutes," he said.

Drayton was pacing up and down nervously; but Sir Charles stood quietly by the window, staring out across the great concrete bowl.

"The problem," murmured Drayton, as if to himself, "is how to get him alone."

"The problem," said Sir Charles softly, without turning, "is how to get him down."

Sir Charles Craig looked at the image on the stereo-screen and said: "Professor Bollinden, I order you to return to Rocket City as soon as your position is favorable for a normal trajectory."

Hervey-Walton and Lord Drayton stood out of range of the eye-panel so that, on the satellite screen, Professor Bollinden would only see the image of the Prime Minister.

The professor smiled. "It is no good, Sir Charles. I have passed the point of no return. You and your colleagues have failed, so the satellite becomes my responsibility."

"You must come down. Nothing can be achieved by this—this madness. You are an intelligent man, Professor Bollinden. Surely you realize that your proposed action will totally destroy all hope of peace?"

"There is none to destroy," said the professor emphatically. "There is only the collective menace of further satellites. But they will never be born, for I shall destroy the Russian and American launching grounds just as I shall destroy Rocket City. Humanity needs more time, and there is only one way of getting it. All space projects, rocket bases and installations must be demolished."

"Where is Dr. Rehn?" asked Sir Charles helplessly.

"He is here." Professor Bollinden stepped aside, and the Austrian scientist took his place.

"Dr. Rehn," said Sir Charles, "do you subscribe to the—er—philosophy of Professor Bollinden?"

"Theoretically, yes," answered Dr. Rehn.

"In practice?" enquired Sir Charles quickly.

"In practice, I would prefer a slight modification."

"What is that?"

"You will see, Sir Charles, when the time comes."

The Austrian moved out of range, and Professor Bollinden resumed his place in front of the eye-panel.

"I will give you four hours to evacuate Rocket City," he

said. "Then I shall destroy it utterly. In an hour, I shall give a similar warning to the Americans at White Sands and Canaveral, and then to the Russians."

"For God's sake come down!" pleaded Sir Charles.

"For God's sake," said the professor, "and for the sake of man, I do what I must." He switched the transceiver off; and over two thousand miles away, his image died on the screen in the Communications Office.

Hervey-Walton immediately tried to re-establish contact, but Lord Drayton said: "It's no use. At that velocity, they'll be out of range. The image was already cloudy. They must be over Southeast Asia by now."

The Prime Minister shrugged. "Perhaps there will be another chance," he said wearily, "in a couple of hours when the satellite has completed a revolution." He gave Drayton a bitter smile. "Here is the inevitable and literal *deus ex machina*. It appears that our little political problems are going to have a surprise solution . . . Well, I suppose Bollinden may be no more insane than we are."

"If only we could get him alone!" exclaimed Drayton impotently.

At that point, Michael Spenser arrived at the Communications Office. The Prime Minister himself explained the situation in a flat, toneless voice.

Time passed inexorably. The Communications Office seemed to possess the atmosphere of the condemned-cell. Drayton sat at the table, doodling nervously with a pencil; Sir Charles Craig had returned to his position by the window; and Michael Spenser divided his time between evolving arguments with which to confront Professor Bollinden and watching the clock.

Presently, the director of Base One, who had been despatched to make emergency arrangements, returned to the office. The Prime Minister turned to him with an enquiring look.

"Everyone is more or less ready for evacuation, Sir Charles . . . I—er—explained that it was part of a very important exercise. I tried to give the impression that it had been thought up by the Brass."

"Did they believe you?"

"I don't know," said Hervey-Walton uncertainly. "It seems to be in the wind that something unusual has happened. The current rumor is that there has been some kind of accident in the orbit—a damaged third-stager to be brought down . . . I didn't deny it too strongly."

"Good man! What about transport?"

"There isn't enough, of course. But I have a convoy of trucks on the way from Base One. They should be here in about half an hour."

"I think we might try to contact the satellite again," said Drayton. "It shouldn't be more than two and a half thousand miles away. We need every minute." He turned to Michael. "You know him as well as anyone, Spenser. Take whatever line you think best—but for heaven's sake make it concise. We have so little time."

"I'm not sure—" began Michael nervously.

"None of us is sure," interrupted the Prime Minister. "And I am already convinced that Lord Drayton or myself would fail. So do your best—and good luck."

"Shall I try to warn him?"

"Only if everything else fails." Then the Prime Minister spoke to the others: "We ought to keep out of range of the eye, gentlemen, and give Mr. Spenser a clear start."

They moved towards the window, while Michael took up position in front of the eye-panel. As he turned the controls, he thought of Mary Bollinden and the cottage in East Anglia. His hand trembled, and beads of moisture formed on his forehead.

Suddenly, the image of Professor Bollinden appeared on the screen.

"Why, hello, Michael! They have sent you to tempt me back, have they?" The professor's smile was strangely equivocal. "What are you going to do—talk about democracy and be sweetly reasonable?"

Seeing the look in his eyes, Michael knew with a quick pity that Professor Bollinden was more than two or three thousand miles away. He was lost in a private world, a valley of grim shadows.

"To hell with democracy," said Micahel in desperation. "I'm thinking of human beings, Dennis, of all the innocent people you are going to kill if you go on with this crazy scheme. What do you want to do—wipe us all out just because you are feeling godlike?"

"I have given ample time for evacuation, Michael," said the professor calmly. "I must say your emotive use of language is unbecoming."

"They won't evacuate," lied Michael. "Drayton says you

are bluffing . . . But if you are not bluffing, God help twenty thousand people!"

Professor Bollinden remained unmoved. "The responsibility lies with Craig. I have informed him of my intentions." He gave a sly smile. "Why don't you ask those two eminent political gentlemen to move into the line of vision? I would like to see their expressions."

"They're not here."

"Be adult, Michael, and be honest. Otherwise I shall switch off."

"Dennis, be human! A few days ago, we were talking about Mary. You said she had more sense than either of us—or both of us put together, for that matter. She has. Do you think she'll be proud of you for holding a pistol to the head of the world?"

"You underestimate Mary," said the professor. "Possibly, she will conclude that this is the sanest thing I have ever done."

"Don't be a fool! This is no answer. What you do to us here will only weaken the Commonwealth. But if you destroy the American and Russian proving grounds, there'll be another global war . . . I'm pleading with you. I'm pleading for Mary and all the women in the world. I'm pleading for the millions of children who, but for this insane scheme of yours, would have at least a fighting chance."

"A fighting chance!" echoed Professor Bollinden satirically. "You do not choose your phrases carefully, Michael. Without me they would have no chance at all, because there would be a three-cornered satellite war. If there is any hope, it lies in the destruction of all satellite bases."

"If there is any hope," said Michael savagely, "it lies in human sanity. Pull yourself together, Dennis, and for God's sake come down! Or let us send a ferry up for you."

"I am in perfect control of myself, thank you," said Professor Bollinden coldly. "If any rocket leaves the launching site, I will vaporize it . . . Don't you think you have done enough grovelling?"

"Wouldn't you prefer me to actually bow down and worship?" demanded Michael bitterly. "At the fountain of absolute knowledge? You ought to give us time to whip up a conclave of cardinals to deify you before we're all blasted to bits! How does it feel to be infallible, Dennis; to know that your decision is absolutely right?"

Looking at the stereo-screen, Michael wondered whether

Professor Bollinden had even heard him, for his eyes seemed curiously remote. It was as if he was no longer watching on his own screen the image of the man in the Communications Office but gazing at some cloudly, inward vision. It was as if he had retired to a private dimension, or had surrendered to a hitherto submerged personality.

"And I beheld when he had opened the sixth seal," intoned the professor, *"and, lo, there was a great earthquake; and the sun became black as sackcloth of hair, and the moon became as blood."*

"You can't do it! You can't do it!" called Michael urgently. "The destruction of the bases won't help, Dennis. That'll bring global war."

But Professor Bollinden no longer heard.

"And the stars of heaven fell unto the earth," he said dreamily, *"even as a fig tree casteth her untimely figs, when she is shaken of a mighty wind."*

"There's something you must know!" shouted Michael. "It's about Otto. He—"

"And the heaven departed as a scroll when it is rolled together; and every mountain and island were moved out of their places."

"Listen, Dennis, listen to me!" coaxed Michael. "That leak over the synchro-pilot gear—Otto had contacts with the Russian Embassy at Canberra! He betrayed us! He's responsible for—"

"And the kings of the earth, and the great men, and the rich men, and the chief captains, and the mighty men, and every bondman, and every free man, hid themselves in the dens and in the rocks of the mountains," came the unheeding, unmoved response.

"He'll trick you, Dennis. He wants the satellite for Russia. Stop him before it's too late!"

"And said to the mountains and rocks, Fall on us, and hide us from the face of Him that sitteth on the throne, and from the wrath of the Lamb."

"Can you hear what I am saying?" demanded Michael frantically. "Can you understand?"

"For the great day of His wrath is come," said Professor Bollinden hypnotically. *"And who shall be able to stand?"*

"You must come down!" repeated Michael with hopeless persistence. "You must stop Otto and come down. He's using you, Dennis. You must—"

Suddenly, Professor Bollinden seemed to recognize again

the man who was talking to him. A smile passed fleetingly over his face.

"Goodbye, Michael," he said gently. "Look after yourself—and do what you can for Mary . . . I shall not reply to any further signals. When the satellite comes round again, I shall beam a Mark Four missile to the launching site. Then Rocket City will return to the desert that gave it birth."

The professor touched a switch; and two thousand miles away in the Communications Office, the stereo-screen became blank.

Michael turned to face the three men who had witnessed that strange battle of words.

"I failed," he said dully.

Sir Charles Craig shook his head. "The failure isn't yours, Michael," he said slowly. "Nor is it wholly Professor Bollinden's. For the last year or two, he has carried a terrible weight of responsibility—carried it in the hope that what he was doing might enable mankind to achieve a new unity of purpose. We have all shared in that responsibility; but none of us, I think, has faced quite so much as he. For, without him, the satellite would never have been . . . He was a fine scientist and a fine man. His—his disintegration is one of the most tragic things I have ever known . . . No, it is not your failure, nor his. It is the failure of a civilization, of a world that offers so little and demands so much."

Gazing at the Prime Minister, hearing him speak, sensing the tremendous tension behind his apparent calm, Michael knew that he, too, was nailed to the cross of a responsibility too great to be carried by a single man. Michael looked at the face of one who was haunted by ghosts, tormented by perpetual nightmares of reality. He looked at the face of a man who wanted to die.

Lord Drayton broke the ensuing silence.

"Well, Charles," he said quietly, "what is to be done?"

With an effort, the Prime Minister pulled himself together. "Evacuate Rocket City," he said wearily. "Get everyone—yourselves included—over to Base One. No one is to remain behind, except myself."

"But—"

"That is an order," said Sir Charles.

"Damn it, you can't stay, Charles," protested Lord Drayton. "Bollinden means what he says. Next time round, he'll drop a Mark Four . . . We can't afford to lose you. It's your duty to—"

"It is my duty to contact the satellite once more and try to avert disaster."

"You heard what Bollinden said, sir," added Hervey-Walton. "He won't acknowledge further signals."

"It is still my duty to try," insisted the Prime Minister.

"You can use the transceiver at Base One, Sir Charles."

"That will not serve my purpose. I, too, must resort to blackmail," said the Prime Minister. "I must attempt to deceive him into thinking that Rocket City has not been evacuated. There is a slender chance that he may hesitate to destroy all the people with whom he has worked."

"I imagine," said Drayton grimly, "that the satellite is no longer controlled by Professor Bollinden. In which case—"

"In which case, I must still make the attempt."

"Sir Charles," said Michael urgently, "let me stay with you. Let me have another try. Perhaps . . ."

The Prime Minister turned to Michael and held out his hand. "Thank you for your co-operation, and your courage." He smiled. "But every man to his own responsibility . . . Mr. Spenser, you will organize and lead the first convoy."

A thousand miles below, the continent of Asia was a solemn merry-go-round. But it was no longer real; for the world had shrunk into a tiny capsule, hanging in space, lost amid the diamond sharpness of the stars.

Aboard Commonwealth Satellite, the two men faced each other. One of them held an automatic pistol firmly: it was pointing at his companion's heart.

Dr. Otto Rehn gazed, with a feeling akin to pity, at the man who was about to die.

"I am sorry, Dennis," he said quietly, "extremely sorry that it must come to this. But I can't let you plunge humanity into the Dark Ages once again. The only hope lies in the unification of the planet. Therefore the nation with the greatest potential must take the lead . . . Your method would merely prolong the race for supremacy."

Professor Bollinden stared at the gun in bewilderment. All his emotional and intellectual power had been stretched to breaking point in the effort necessary to fulfil his self-given task—the destruction of the rocket launching sites, the proving grounds and bases of the three great powers. Here, now, was the one possibility he had not considered. He felt neither fear nor anger, for there was no strength left.

"So it was true!" he said hoarsely. "It was you. Otto, who was selling us out—destroying the time margin."

The Austrian grimaced. "Not selling out, Dennis. I am neither a mercenary nor a communist."

"Why the devil did you do it?" Professor Bollinden gazed at him with childlike incredulity.

Dr. Rehn gave a thin smile. "The devil may have had something to do with it," he conceded. "At least, the Old Testament devil, whom I interpret as the first seeker after knowledge, and therefore the first scientist. His experiment with Adam and Eve was most interesting. We now have its logical conclusion."

"Don't prevaricate, Otto," said the professor, unexpectedly regaining a little composure. "There is no time for satire. In a moment or so, you will be forced to press the trigger."

"Why?"

"Because," answered Professor Bollinden calmly, "I am mad and I know that I am mad; so I am in no mood to countenance indecision . . . Why did you sell out?"

"The principle of the universality of knowledge," suggested the Austrian lightly.

"Stop being a fool!"

"Very well, Dennis, I will tell you. I sold out—as you call it—for the same reason that I am taking control of this satellite. You remarked some time ago that we should have spent our declining years studying social history."

"So?"

"So, Dennis, that has been my preoccupation for some years. And I have realized that humanity will never be able to get on with its true task until the world is one world; until a single ideology is strong enough, and has sufficient resources, to dominate all others."

"What about democracy?"

"Democracy is dying. It carries the seeds of its own decay. The Commonwealth is too weak, and America is too erratic. Only Russia—under the so-called communist regime—has sufficient staying power, sufficient energy to bind the world together . . . I do not believe in communism, Dennis, but I believe—as any scientist should—in the unity of the species. That is why this satellite must be used by Russia. And that is why—"

"It seems you, too, wish to control the course of natural selection," interrupted the professor wearily. "I think this project, under the conditions we have had to endure, has made us all succumb to paranoia."

"I do not propose to control," said the Austrián. "I shall merely accelerate. Control by Russia is the logical conclusion . . . You, unfortunately, forced my hand."

Professor Bollinden shrugged. "What do you intend to do?"

Unconsciously, Dr. Rehn lowered the pistol as he considered his reply. "A modified version of your own plan would be admirable. I shall destroy Rocket City and the American proving grounds and bases. Then I shall communicate with the Soviets, and endeavor to hold on until they are able to—"

But Professor Bollinden had already launched himself across the small chamber in an attempt to regain control.

He was not quick enough. The pistol jerked up and a bullet tore into his chest. A look of sheer amazement spread over his face; and then his knees buckled slowly.

Dr. Rehn threw the gun down and knelt by the man with whom he had worked for so long. Gently, he turned him over and pillowed the professor's head upon his arm. The glaze of death was already creeping into the scientist's eyes.

"Forgive me, Dennis. It was—necessary."

Professor Bollinden gave a grim smile. "Yes . . . it would be." His voice was no more than a whisper. The words came with a terrible effort. "And so . . . the world . . . belongs to —to Mephistopheles!"

He coughed once, painfully, and then his body slackened.

Curiously enough, it was then, for the first time, as cold theory became translated into stark fact, that Dr. Otto Rehn knew the meaning of despair.

He lifted his head and gazed out through the plastiglass window at a silent, spinning world; at a vault of hard, unwinking stars . . .

President Hudson gazed at the decoded radiogram. He did not take long to make up his mind, for the first thing he realized was that every minute was vital. He touched a button on his desk, and a presidential aide appeared as if by magic.

The aide saw that the President's hands were trembling and that his face had taken on a greyish pallor; but he did not betray any sign of noticing such things, since he was trained to notice nothing unless he was so required.

"Take this down and get it off," said President Hudson.

"Yes, sir." A pad and stylo appeared—again magically—in the aide's hand.

"Most secret, most urgent, priority one," dictated the President. "To Missile Command: Fit triple-H warheads to all single or multi-stage vehicles with homing device capable of matching velocity Commonwealth Satellite. Saturate orbit. Attack until destroyed. Effective immediately. Do not accept countermand. President direct. End of message."

The aide galvanized into activity like an automaton. He did not know it, but his features already wore the same greyish tinge as the President's.

Within minutes, Boris Marienkov, First Secretary of the Communist Party of the Soviet Union, was aware of President Hudson's decision. His heavy brow became furrowed, and his thick moustache seemed to droop further over his lower lip.

Comrade Marienkov was fortunate in possessing the same type of massive body and ponderous features as that distinguishied predecessor who, long ago, had routed the Nazi armies striking at the heart of the Soviet Union. It had made his process of self-identification easier and—invoking a kind of defensive superstition among his colleagues—had facilitated his rise in the Party.

"Now," he asked himself silently, "what would the Old Bear have done?"

The general who had brought the news and was now awaiting orders stood stiffly before Comrade Marienkov's desk.

At length, the First Secretary looked up and smiled.

"Let them," he said. "Commonwealth Satellite is expendable."

"But, Comrade Marienkov, the Austrian scientist has—"

"The Austrian scientist has made a fool of himself. And a fool is dangerous to everyone. His destruction is insignificant; but the destruction of Commonwealth Satellite—if the Americans are successful—will provide the best propaganda weapon we have had for decades. And even if they do not succeed in eliminating the satellite, then we are in an even stronger position. Our own satellite will be operational very soon now."

"That is so, Comrade. Meanwhile?"

"Meanwhile," said Comrade Marienkov, "the correct procedure would be to program all intercontinental missiles on the northern perimeter for their targets, and have the Polar Division in readiness for immediate action."

"Do you think, in view of the American action, that this may be regarded as the beginning?"

The First Secretary assumed his most genial, bearlike expression. "Frankly, General, I think it may be more properly regarded as the end."

One thousand miles above the Pacific Ocean, a tiny mobile star burst silently into a brief and incredibly bright radiance.

It was like a signal, a transient beacon. Then the darkness swallowed it.

But soon, on the surface of the earth below, it was answered by similar beacons—bright signals of destruction. The bitter harvest of fire yielded by continent after continent, heralding the tragic autumn of terrestrial man.

Part Two

To everything there is a season, and a time to every purpose under the heaven:

A time to be born, and a time to die; a time to plant and a time to pluck up that which is planted;

A time to kill, and a time to heal; a time to break down and a time to build up . . .

ECCLESIASTES

. . . But it does not at present look as though Nature had designed the universe primarily for life; the normal star and the normal nebula have nothing to do with life except making it impossible. Life is the end of a chain of by-products; it seems to be the accident, and torrential deluges of life-destroying radiation the essential.

There is a temptation to base wide-reaching inferences on the fact that the universe as a whole is apparently antagonistic to life.

SIR JAMES JEANS: EOS

THE SEED

Proem

Nature herself pointed the way. Once in the green fields of Earth, when autumn's coppery glow settled over a mellow landscape, it was possible to watch the moment of life and death explode upon the tranquil certainty of resurrection.

It was possible to watch the tiny brittle seed-cases of vanished flowers crackle with urgency in the morning sunlight, scattering their seed in blind acceptance of the hazards of rock, clay, sunless corners or the hunger of birds; seeking the dark and ultimate promise of the soil.

But as the childlike lord of the planet, the human animal, continued to amuse himself with his latest toy—with the secret of a terrible fire stolen from the threshold of existence—the established rhythms were displaced; the seasons merged; the jungles retreated; deserts became stagnant lakes; the oceans of the world were choked by floating islands of fish that were dead or dying; plantation and prairie, forest and farmland turned gray, then black, as the vegetation crumbled to a lifeless powder. And finally, the soil died.

The Earth itself was a withered flower whose last duty lay in the propagation of the seed, the scattering of tiny capsules of life among the indifferent stars.

And the seed was of hope and despair, of creation and destruction, of poetry and madness. It was all the stricken planet had to offer—its own destroyer—a few specimens of the mammal whose gift of language had enabled it to style itself, with no small irony, *homo sapiens*.

There was no alternative, for Man was the last survivor. A fugitive from the poisoned air, the poisoned soil and the poisoned water, he still clung desperately to life in the half dozen outposts that were the remnants of his global civilization. Day by day, in those cities whose transparent plastic domes still held back the gathering tide of death, he worked with the frenzied purpose of the doomed.

For, having destroyed the terrestrial future of his race, he sought a new unsullied world, a new beginning. He dreamed of another virgin planet where the old mistakes might be avoided, where the new knowledge might be increased.

So, in a fever of anxiety, with no time and no resources for experiment or consolidation, he began to build ships for an impossible voyage, the perils of which would only be equalled by not making it at all.

Wasting no effort on the rest of the solar planets, which he already knew were incapable of supporting him, Man set himself the task of building starships, and the penance of unimaginable journeys through the void.

Survival had assumed the proportions of a religion—which was fitting and, indeed, necessary; for it is one thing to contemplate the star-voyage and another to make it.

But what sort of faith would sustain such a restless animal through years of imprisonment, through decades of darkness, through the overwhelming silence of drifting centuries?

And what would it all come to in the end?

Chapter One

Firing Point

The situation in Europe Three, the largest of the five cities that remained on a dead continent, was much the same as elsewhere. Men and women murdered and died for it; they pleaded and blackmailed for it; they plotted and competed for it—for the slender hope of survival, the promise of at least one small chance, offered to those who would presently leave the planet in their starship.

In Europe One, the problem had already been solved, providing a grim warning for the rest. The Scientific Administration, the ship-builders who had become the last legitimate regime, were overthrown by violence. The ringleaders, naturally, were men whose applications for the star-flight had been rejected. But this last revolution was no different from any since the dawn of history: it was easier to begin than to stop.

Canalizing the mass-hysteria of the mass-condemned, the citizens of Europe One destroyed the unfinished starship; and in doing so, ruptured the city's protective dome. The gaps were not large enough to be unduly dangerous. If the city's repair service had not been disorganized, they might have been dealt with satisfactorily in half a day.

But death was no longer waiting outside: death had already entered. Machine-guns chattered briskly in the streets, and were answered by the staccato bark of carbines, the explosive laughter of grenades. And for many human beings, this noisy argument of steel was the last they ever heard, the first they ever understood.

Several repair workers, acting on their own initiative, were even shot down as they tried to close the gaps in the transparent dome. Presently, no one dared to make the attempt; and presently the city realized that the final bogeyman had come to claim all the naughty children, had come to put the city quietly to sleep. For the unseen poison drifted through the gaps like an invisible wraith, probing with soft and deadly fingers into lungs that could feel no warning pain.

Then flesh began to turn gray, and eyes darkened. And the people of Europe One knew that there was little time left. It was common knowledge—an infant of three could have recited the fact—that the poisoned air took no more than seven days to kill.

So the problem was solved. Nobody from Europe One would ever voyage among the stars. One of the few precious Earth-seeds had been destroyed in the making.

Seven days to zero. Suddenly the people became stunned and silent. Then some began to cry, and some to laugh; some began to make love, and some to get drunk; some cut their throats, and some curled up quietly like tired babies, seeking the comfort of the foetal attitude, the oblivion of prebirth.

At last there were no more radio signals from Europe One. The transformation into a necropolis was complete.

It was a grim warning, and the Administrators of the remaining cities did their best to profit by it. For all civilians, the possession of a lethal weapon was itself an offence punishable by death. It was also prohibited for groups of more than a dozen people to gather anywhere at any time. Candidates for the star-flight, whose applications had been rejected, were now automatically imprisoned, to be released only when the starship was under way. Successful candidates also—whose incidence of mortality and illness had become sufficiently high to make a successful application itself seem like a death sentence—were now placed under a triple guard, beyond the reach of jealousy, frustration and a resentment born of sheer despair.

In Europe Three, the shipyard was surrounded by a ring of electrically controlled strongpoints whose combined firepower could, if necessary, annihilate the entire population. But even this was not enough; for half a dozen of the very scientists who had conceived the starship entered an abortive plot to seize it for their own purposes. Being well over thirty, the upper age limit for star-voyagers, they forgot their duty to the race and saw in the gleaming ship only a means of escaping their own fate—the ultimate victory of the poisoned elements.

The conspiracy was premature, and its leaders were defeated. They were too valuable to be executed; but henceforth they were forced to continue their work alone, each with a pistol at his back and a younger scientist at his side to check the validity of results.

No one of technical or scientific ability could be wasted; and no one was entirely incorruptible. For every three men who worked there was one who watched, and for every three watchers there was another watcher, the combinations being changed from day to day.

Miraculously, the starship continued to grow, a tapering column of hiduminium and steel; a triumph of human ingenuity; a monument to human weakness; a seed of infinite beauty.

The citizens of Europe Three watched it grow with pride and fear, with hatred and with hope. It was good to belong to a race capable of such an achievement; but then there was the bitter knowledge that men had only created this machine in order to run away. There was also another aspect of the starship, which directly concerned every living being in the city: a problem the enormity of which was realized chiefly by the men of the dome repair service.

The bow of the starship already rose like a silver steeple beyond the transparent dome into the poisoned outer atmosphere. A double cavity trap had been built round the neat circular hole so that none of the air rendered lethal by radioactivity could enter the city. But when or *if* the starship ever rose into space, the cavity trap would be destroyed; the heat and vibration might even cause the entire dome to collapse.

At best, the ship's departure would enable several million cubic meters of poisoned air to rush in before the gap could be closed: at worst, it would leave Europe Three with less than seven days of disintegrating life. It seemed probable that the ancient law would be fulfilled; that the scattering of the seed would be achieved only by the destruction of the seed-case.

There were many who, understandably, did not wish to risk the remaining months of life for such a venture. What was it to them that mankind should seek a new home, hidden behind a misty unimaginable curtain of light-years? As the starship neared completion, its ring of guns and high tension wires was ominously strengthened.

The star-voyagers, who were glad to risk a quick death for

the sake of hope in preference to a slow death without any hope, called their ship *Solarian* to commemorate the group of planets and the parent sun they were leaving for ever. But those who were to remain behind preferred a more emotive connotation. To them, the ship was Nemesis.

The *Solarian* was a hundred meters high and, at its broadest point, twenty meters in diameter. It was designed to carry an initial crew of ten people only, with provision for subsequent children, yet in that vast hull every cubic meter of space was indispensable; for the ship was a self-contained world which might be required to support human life independently for centuries.

It was powered by volatility rockets and sub-atomic motors. Its shape was conventional, but there were retractile fins with aerodynamic controls. Thus it would be able to cruise in space and yet maneuver in atmosphere. When in starflight, it would cruise for years on the power drawn from a single liter of water, or transmute and use the radiant energy of the nearest sun. When in planetary drive, its volatility rockets would use the substance of the atmosphere through which it journeyed.

Provision had been made for everything aboard—air, water and all organic material—to be re-cycled indefinitely in a closed circuit, thus eliminating the waste of any precious biological matter.

The ten people who had been selected to voyage in the *Solarian* were the best that the doomed city of Europe Three could offer. They were, by all measurable standards, the élite.

In order to be considered for the star-voyage, a man had to be between twenty-five and thirty years of age, and a woman between twenty-three and twenty-five. But the prime necessity was that each must be physically sound and fertile; for there would be no point in reaching an hospitable planet if the discoverers could not procreate.

In fact, the complement of the *Solarian* was not to be regarded as ten individuals but as five sexual pairs, each willing to produce or limit offspring to the numbers made necessary by circumstance.

After such a basic need came the lesser qualifications. Each member of the expedition must have an Intelligence Quotient of not less than a hundred and thirty-five, and the stamina/endurance ratio of an all-round athlete. Each must be a master or mistress of at least two, preferably three, professional skills or sciences; and the manual dexterity of all must be equal to any task in store—whether pioneering or painting, whether farming or fighting for sheer life.

Finally, each must regard himself no longer as a separate entity, an independent personality, but as part of a life-unit —a nucleus that might one day expand into a tribe; that might, phoenixlike, bring forth a new human race.

Symbolic of this personal surrender, each member, on being accepted for the expedition, took a new name—one that would be a constant reminder of something more lasting than mere personality, an inspiration to new effort and a memorial for a vanished civilization.

The man who took the name of Newton came to be elected leader of the expedition. He was a quiet, forceful man of twenty-nine; an astro-physicist whose subsidiary study was sociology. His superficial absentmindedness concealed an ability to make lightning decisions and enforce them with a disarming smile—which was no small asset in the role he had accepted.

His partner was Roma, a vivacious brunette of twenty-five, who had studied genetics and ecology. In direct contrast to Newton's air of premature age, Roma was ebullient and unselfconscious: a natural antithesis. One day they hoped to see children growing up on a planet where it was unnecessary to seal out poisoned air. One day they hoped to see the star-born nucleus of a new *homo sapiens*.

Second in command to Newton was Lavoisier, the twenty-seven year old chemist and geologist. His personality was more impressive, more clearly defined than Newton's; but somehow less dominant. He was partnered with Troy, a slender, serious girl four years younger, who specialized in hydroponics and child education.

The oldest member of the unit was Jung, whose age had almost disqualified him. He was approaching thirty-one. But Jung was irreplaceable, combining as he did the duties of surgeon, physician and psychiatrist. In many ways, he was the most remarkable member of the group, his integrity and intellectual superiority being unquestioned. However, his natural role was not that of leader but of detached observer and general counsellor. He was the life-unit's substitute for a tribal wise man. Vienne, a blonde twenty-four-year-old anthropologist and historian was an admirable partner for him. Like Jung, but in a much lesser way, she, too, was emotionally detached—except in their personal relationship.

Rilke, a muscular and vaguely unpredictable man of twenty-eight, co-ordinated the various departments of biology. His partner, Alexandria, was the ship's librarian, photographer and purser. Being just twenty-three, she was the youngest of the group; but at times her curious air of gravity made her seem a good deal older.

Finally, there was Socrates and Athene, aged twenty-nine and twenty-five. Socrates was a hard-headed electronics engineer, responsible for mechanical installations, servo-mechanisms and power maintenance. Athene, a dark sultry woman, was dietician and also in charge of the re-cycling plant.

The ten members of the life-unit made the *Solarian* their permanent home thirty days before the agreed firing point. They needed as much time as possible to accustom themselves to the environment, topography and mechanical intricacies of the starship.

Having made their farewells, they were then cut off forever from the rest of the human race, as the massive entry-port was sealed. Routine radio messages came to them, and occasionally they would climb up into the astrodome to look down on the world outside; but already they felt themselves to be exiles—a group whose destiny separated them emotionally and physically from the doomed species.

As the days went by, and the group became oriented in its new surroundings and duties, tension mounted—both within the *Solarian* and outside it. For as firing point approached, so also did the citizens of Europe Three approach breaking point.

The defensive ring still lay round the starship; but sabotage was becoming more frequent—and more successful. It was only a matter of time before the ring became impotent, and then it would remain to be seen whether Europe Three was prepared to risk its remaining months of existence for the preservation of the seed.

Five days before the scheduled firing point, Newton called a meeting in the ship's dining-room/council-chamber. He wasted no time on preliminaries.

"The situation outside is critical," he announced curtly.

"We've had our warning," observed Jung. "Europe Three is just discovering what the departure of the *Solarian* will mean . . . Pretty soon, they'll even forget what happened in Europe One."

"Exactly," agreed Newton. "The high tension wires are down and the first ring has been broken. City Control says they don't want to take action unless they're forced to, because it might touch off a riot."

"Can they destroy the ship?" asked Troy.

Socrates gave a thin smile. "No—but they can make it unspaceworthy."

"At a time like this," remarked Vienne coolly, "the popular sentiment becomes: 'We can only die once, and we all ought to die together.' "

"Which passes the baby to us," added Newton. "It's a nice problem."

There was almost a minute's silence. The ten members of the life-unit looked at each other uncertainly.

It was Jung who spoke first. "In five days, the dome repair service will have to cope with the wrecked cavity trap when we have cleared the city. We all know there isn't much chance, but there is *some*. If we don't wreak too much havoc, they might just manage to close the gap before the critical volume has entered . . . But in their present mood, it doesn't look as if the population will wait five days. However, things are a little different here than they were in Europe One. Our starship is complete. The decision rests not with the people outside, but with the *Solarian's* life unit."

"I can supply power for take-off in less than thirty minutes," said Socrates.

"If we leave before time," remarked Troy hesitantly, "it amounts to passing the death sentence on them."

"The death sentence has already been passed," observed Lavoisier with a somber smile. "We would merely advance the execution date. Personally, I believe in the larger issues at stake. Earth is dying, but it's our duty to see that mankind doesn't die with it. Other starships may leave the remaining cities, but we have to act as if ours is the only one. We must assume that the future—if any—of *homo sapiens* depends entirely on us."

Roma gave an exasperated sigh. "It boils down to the old problem. Does the end justify the means?"

"That's the point," remarked Jung. "Most of us believe that the end doesn't justify the means, but we usually act as if it does."

Rilke shrugged. "Personally, I don't think we can afford

the luxury of ethics just now." He looked at Newton expectantly.

But Newton shook his head. "This is not my decision only: it belongs to us all . . . Please raise your hands if you think we should take off as soon as there is any serious threat."

Slowly, very slowly, ten hands were raised. Newton's was the last.

"That's that," he said briskly. A rueful smile came to his lips as he gazed at his companions. "There really wasn't any choice at all, was there?"

No one answered.

Socrates broke the silence. "I'll need four people to help me check the Block A fuel feed and the secondary distributors. Also I'll try to fix the synchro-ignition for minimum rise velocity. If they make us leave before time, we'll do as little damage as possible."

"You can have Lavoisier, Roma, Vienne and Rilke," said Newton. "I want Alexandria and Jung to keep watch in the astrodome. They can observe the whole firing area from there. Athene will keep radio contact with City Control, and Troy will check the contour-berths . . . If anyone wants me, I shall be on the observation catwalk, or else the navigation deck."

As soon as he had finished, the members of the life-unit dispersed to their appointed tasks.

Alexandria pressed the intercom switch and spoke to Newton on the navigation deck. "They are coming," she warned. "Several hundred on the North Avenue."

"Thanks. I've seen them," answered Newton. "Socrates will give them a warning blast on the auxiliary rockets."

At the radio panel, Athene stopped signalling, listened intently for a few seconds, then switched in to Newton: "City Control doesn't reply. I've been trying them for the last ten minutes."

"All right," said Newton. "Stand by. In a few minutes, I'll probably want everyone on the navigation deck—with the exception of Socrates."

He looked at the external visulator. The large bright screen gave a clear image of the *Solarian* against a background of the remaining constructional debris and the two supply avenues that converged on the firing area.

From the navigation deck, it seemed as if a disorderly swarm of ants made its way slowly along the North Avenue.

But it was not a swarm of ants: it was an angry, perplexed, frightened mass of human beings who achieved unity only in their lust for destruction. Newton watched their advance, fascinated. The temperature on the navigation deck was normal; but there were beads of sweat on his forehead.

Socrates' voice came over the intercom: "The auxiliaries are ready . . . They ought not to come any nearer—for their own sakes."

Newton hesitated for a moment. "Give them a five second blast."

"Here it comes," announced Socrates. "Five, four, three, two, one—out!"

Briefly, the *Solarian* quivered with a high-pitched humming. Green flames—spectacular, but not as yet dangerous to the oncoming citizens—belched from the auxiliary tubes. The mass of people seemed to freeze, then expand, as they flung themselves flat on the ground in a panic.

The flames died; the humming subsided. As the crowd angrily picked itself up and began to surge forward again, Newton's voice came to them over a series of amplifiers:

"Go back to your homes peacefully. You can't destroy the starship. Be patient, and in five more days the *Solarian* will leave. There will be a greater chance of safety when the dome repair service is ready to deal with the gap. If you force us to leave now, the damage may be irreparable . . . Go home and be patient . . . We are risking our own lives, too."

The crowd swayed indecisively. Then someone threw a grenade which fell harmlessly short. But the flash of its explosion became a signal. A shower of grenades followed, then small arms opened up; and the hull of the *Solarian* began to sing with the impact of futile bullets.

Newton sighed, laid down the hand microphone, and switched in all departments of the ship on the intercom.

"If we stay any longer, we endanger the project . . . Everyone, except Socrates and myself, will now go to their contour-berths on the navigation deck . . . Socrates, give them a ten second blast, and trigger the take-off tubes for departure within five minutes."

Once more, the high-pitched humming began; and temporarily the shower of missiles directed against the ship thinned out as the crowd took cover. Meanwhile, the members of the life-unit hurried to obey their leader, who was already checking the manual controls, setting the electrochron, and feeding the automatic take-off ribbon to the main electronic co-ordinator.

The ten-second blast ended, and the bombardment was resumed. Newton spoke once more to the crowd over the shipyard system of amplifiers, making a last appeal, warning them that the starship was preparing to take off. But grenades and small arms fire destroyed the amplifiers before he could complete his message; and the attack was intensified.

Eight members of the life-unit gazed expectantly at their leader, standing now in the semi-circle of contour-berths.

He shrugged. "Reason versus emotion. Will it always be like that?"

Lavoisier gave the answer. "On this planet—yes. We have to find a world where reason gets another chance."

"Where reason and emotion may become allies," added Jung, "instead of enemies."

Newton glanced at the electrochron, and at the same time Socrates spoke over the intercom: "Take-off tubes all set, auxiliaries synchronized . . . Anything more?"

"Come up to your berth," replied Newton. "Firing point is in less than two minutes." He pressed the master-switch, activating the electrochron, and climbed into his own contour-berth. A few seconds later, Socrates reached the navigation deck. Ten pairs of eyes were fixed on the red sweeping hand of the electrochron.

Outside, the bombardment became stronger. A dull, heavy explosion caused the ship to quiver slightly. The ten star-voyagers exchanged anxious glances.

"It wasn't the ship," said Socrates confidently. "Must be the blockhouses."

Another explosion reverberated, then there was a brief lull. In the sudden silence, the voice of the ship's auto-announcer bomed its apocalyptic message:

"Sixty seconds to firing point!"

"Goodbye, Earth," whispered Roma, half to herself. "You put up with the human race a long time—too long, perhaps."

"Forty-five seconds to firing point!"

"Europe Three," said Troy. "Home . . . No matter what happens, we won't forget."

"Thirty seconds to firing point!"

With a faint smile, Newton spoke his last words on earth: "Through difficulty to the stars . . . It used to be the motto of British airmen."

"Fifteen seconds to firing point!" said the auto-announcer. *"Ten, nine, eight, seven, six, five, four, three, two, one—zero!"*

The starship came to life. A vibration so powerful, so high that it completely bypassed auditory detection, rippled through the straining *Solarian*. The green flames of the take-off tubes turned blue, then blinding white, immediately transforming the still advancing tide of humanity into a scattering, terror-stricken mob.

Almost imperceptibly, the sleek hundred-meter column rose clear of its launching site; and at the same time, unobserved, its ominous noise drowned in the roar of rockets, the cavity trap was ripped away, and fragments of the city's plastic dome fell like surrealist hail over the shipyard.

A moment later, and the *Solarian* was clear of Europe Three, relentlessly accelerating as it drove up through the thinning layers of poisoned atmosphere, up towards the dark and timeless brilliance of space.

The starship was invisible before its attackers had recovered themselves sufficiently to look. They saw only the jagged, smouldering forty-meter gap left by its transit, the fantastic cracks that even yet appeared to be spreading. And then they felt a cold, deadly breeze as the lethal air poured in.

Low animal cries, increasing in volume, rose from thousands of throats as an invisible wave of panic swept through the city. In their homes, men bolted doors and windows, women drew the curtains and called anxiously for reassurance, hoping for some last-minute miracle to delay the inevitable end.

But the virus of panic spread more swiftly than any physical disease. Soon the city was powerless in its grip.

Presently, the grim drama of Europe One began to unfold itself once more. Rapine and violence, despair and fatalism, spreading under their own inexorable laws, made futile all the laws of man.

Europe Three was dying; but unlike Europe One, there was a purpose in its death, a fulfilment even in its destruction.

For the seed had been shot out towards the stars: the seed-case had not failed its destiny.

Chapter Two

The First Year

Roma was in the *Solarian's* nursery, staring dully at an empty cot which bore the unmistakable signs of recent occupation. It was one of six. The two to the left of it contained Atlanta, the three-months' old daughter of Lavoisier and Troy; and Zeno, the month-old son of Jung and Vienne. The remaining cots had not yet been used.

In less than ten weeks, Roma herself would give birth to a child. Then there would be three star-children. But at the moment, there was no pleasure in anticipation.

Hearing a sound behind her, she turned and saw Alexandria, pale and drawn, leaning against the bulkhead. Thin rivulets shone against the whiteness of her cheeks.

"Where is he?" whispered Alexandria.

Roma put an arm round her shoulder. "Why don't you go and have a rest, my dear? You mustn't exert yourself—not yet."

"Where is he?"

"Please," coaxed Roma. "You'll feel stronger in a few hours. It's far too soon to be walking about . . . Let me get you a couple of sleeping tablets, then we'll have a little chat before you drop off."

Alexandria swayed, and her voice became momentarily distant: "Where is my son?"

"I . . . I do wish you wouldn't make it harder for yourself."

"Don't you see? I've got to know! *I must know!*" Her voice rose hysterically.

Roma's knuckles whitened as she nerved herself for the inevitable. "Poor Alexandria," she said. "You know already, don't you?"

"He—he was a Mongoloid, wasn't he?"

Roma nodded. There was pity in her eyes.

"What have you done with him?"

"Please let me take you back. You mustn't get excited . . . I can imagine how you feel—it's heartbreaking. But in another year . . ." Her words ended lamely.

"Another year! Another year of this damned star-flight! Another year of maddening stillness! What do I care about it? I don't care one straw—one single bloody straw. We're not a life-unit; we're a sample of canned biology—a bowl of idiot goldfish . . . Where is my son, Roma? Please let me see him—just once more . . . *Please!*" The perspiration stood on her forehead. Soon she would reach breaking-point.

Roma watched her, waiting for the tell-tale signs of collapse; knowing that for Alexandria's sake she must force the pace.

"We're all desperately sorry," she said, "because in a way he belonged to us all . . . But—but try to remember what we agreed before *Solarian* left Europe Three."

"And what did we agree?" It was Jung's voice. Unheard by the two women, he had come along the passageway from the upper deck, and stood watching them.

Alexandria turned to him. "They won't let me see my baby—I only want to see him once more, and they won't let me . . . Please make them understand . . . Just once, that's all."

Jung watched her, noting the symptoms. "There is your baby, Alexandria." He pointed to one of the cots. "Take him. In a little while, he will be hungry."

"No! Zeno belongs to you and Vienne. I want my own baby."

"There is your baby. Take him."

"Can't you understand? I want my own."

Jung took her hands in his, and looked steadily into her eyes. "He was ours, too, Alexandria—just as Zeno is yours . . . We are not normal families. We can't afford to be. For better or worse, we are simply a life-unit—yes, I know, a sample of canned biology! But there can be good samples and bad. Help us to make it a good one: we need your help—all of it, all the time . . . It's the same for each of us; and it isn't easy, is it? I, too, have lost my son . . ."

"*You* haven't lost your son!"

"Yes, I have. He wasn't destined for the star-flight. For him, the journey would have been meaningless, the destination futile . . . He was a Mongoloid type, and therefore he died."

"Oh, God!" She forced back the tears, and a bitter edge came to her voice. "He wasn't yours, so you let them kill him."

"You were his mother, and Rilke his father; but he belonged to me and Vienne, to Newton and Roma. He belonged to us all. So do Zeno and Atlanta . . . As we suffer the loss of the baby that died, so you must accept the happiness of the star-children that live."

"You let them kill him!"

"No, I allowed him to die myself. We would all have given him our love. But the star-flight would have been too much for him. He needed more than love. He needed oblivion."

Alexandria choked the inevitable accusation, and tried to control herself: "I do understand—really . . . It's just that I still want to see him—only this once. I . . . I want to remember him."

Jung shook his head. "I'm sorry," he said gently, "but it was better for you and for us all that the task was completed quickly."

Slowly, the implication of his words sank in. Alexandria felt a sudden coldness grip her. "Re-cycled!" The word was less than a whisper. Yet it was as if it had been shouted. It was at once an accustation and an epitaph.

"Is that so terrible?" asked Roma softly.

Jung made the terror-stricken girl meet his gaze. "All living things sustain each other. All living things depend upon death not as an end, an absolute completion, but as the beginning of a new rhythm, a way of fulfilment in passing on the restless force of life . . . Earth, itself, was a closed biological system. The dead always sustain the living, and are re-cycled into different patterns of life . . . That is the function of death."

There was no warning at all. Alexandria's head fell loosely forward, and her body suddenly slackened in his arms.

Jung glanced at Roma. "I'll take her," he said. "You had better warn Rilke . . . She needs about twenty hours' sleep; and then I might try psycho-narcosis."

"Will she be all right?"

He smiled. "The human spirit can take more than you think." Carrying Alexandria's limp body with ease, he went out of the nursery and along the passageway.

Newton leaned back in his chair and looked at Lavoisier

thoughtfully: "Nearly a quarter of a light-year. Four hundred days ago, I would have said it was impossible."

Lavoisier gave him an ironic smile. "It's nice to have practice improve on theory for a change. How long do you think it will take—twenty years?"

Newton shook his head: "Allowing for deceleration beginning somewhere between the twelfth and fifteenth year, we ought to reach Alpha Centauri between the twenty-fifth and thirtieth."

Lavoisier chuckled: "A nice accurate calculation!"

"Sorry to be so vague, but I really haven't a clue. The continuing possibility of acceleration has upset all my preconceived ideas. We might even make it before the second generation reaches maturity. On the other hand, it might not be until our grandchildren's time . . . Personally, I would like to play safe and try a practice deceleration in deep space—say for about six months. It wouldn't lose a great deal of time, and it would give me some valuable data."

"Why not put the idea to Socrates?" suggested Lavoisier.

Newton shrugged: "I have already sounded him. He doesn't think very much of it."

"Any particular reason?"

"Eager for landfall, I suppose He has an. unshakeable confidence that Alpha Centauri will present us with a convenient system of planets."

"What a hope!"

"I know . . . It's difficult to stay on the knife edge between optimism and pessimism. I suppose we are all unwilling to surrender our personal daydreams; but even before we left Earth it was made perfectly clear that the present generation might find itself sentenced to perpetual starflight."

"Speaking of Earth," said Lavoisier slowly, "I wonder what it's like there now?"

"Extremely peaceful," answered Newton drily, "now that the destroyer has departed or been destroyed."

"You think it will be all over by now?"

"Don't you?"

"I suppose so; but it's difficult to imagine total death . . . What's your guess about Europe Three?"

"When we left?"

"Yes."

Newton looked at him curiously. "I know what happened to Europe Three. I saw it on the main visulator—for about half a second . . . We made a hell of a gap, then the dome began to crack."

"And you kept it to yourself for over a year!" Lavoisier sounded reproachful.

A wintry smile settled on Newton's face. "Hardly the sort of glad tidings one spreads with joy . . . It seemed expedient to let the others form their own conclusions . . . Besides, nobody likes to feel they have executed a city—I can make *that* statement with authority!"

"Q.E.D.," said Lavoisier calmly. "I like to keep the records straight . . . The reality is beginning to recede now. In another year or two, it won't mean anything emotionally: it will be just another item in the Journal."

"Yes," said Newton, standing up. "Just another item in the Journal." He went to a locker and took out a combination pressure suit.

"Where are you off to, now?"

"I thought I'd take a stroll on the hull."

"Socrates did the routine inspection yesterday."

"I know . . . I just have an old-fashioned urge to count the stars."

Sol was still the most brilliant of all; but imperceptibly, as the star-flight developed, as the *Solarian* increased velocity over the days, months and years, another star would assume that distinction; and then another. Eventually, it would be difficult to decide off-hand which of all those hard bright points, set against the backcloth of complete darkness, possessed a planet that had once nurtured *homo sapiens*.

Gazing through the plastiglass visor of his headpiece, Newton sighed, trying to visualize the rich contours of Earth—more than a million million miles away. Already, it had acquired the dimensions of a legend. Soon, especially for the second generation, it would have all the emotive connotation of a myth—at one with Parnassus, Valhalla, Eden, the Islands of the Blest.

To those who were doomed to spend the major part of their lives journeying through the dark and meaningless silence, with only the slow brightening and dimming of stars to mark the illusion of progress, Earth would shed its harsh reality, its history of violence, and become a sempiternal paradise.

A Paradise Lost . . .

Standing on the outside hull of the *Solarian* was like standing at the still, mathematical center of the star-pricked ball of space. It produced illusions of grandeur and insignificance —illusions of meaning. It released a torrent of sensations that were difficult to bear, and certainly could not be borne for long.

Before he went back to the entry-port, Newton picked out Alpha Centauri and gazed at it steadily for a few seconds.

Would it or any other star be hospitable enough to offer a planet whose surface bore some resemblance to the continents and oceans, the hills and fertile valleys of Earth?

And if so, would it be possible for the new race to avoid what, in retrospect, had been inevitable—Hiroshima, New York, London, Moscow, Europe Three?

Desperately, he tried not to think.

Only to hope.

Chapter Three

The Fifth Year

"What is a tree?" demanded Zeno, his infant face registering great concentration. "You told me what a king was, but you didn't tell me about a tree."

"I'll show you one," said Troy. She went to the schoolroom locker and selected a micro-film strip. Slipping it into the projector, she pressed the control pin, and the image of an oak tree in full leaf flashed upon the meter-wide screen. Zeno and Atlanta gazed at it.

"What a funny animal," said Atlanta slowly. "Does it bite?"

Troy shook her head and smiled. "It's a plant—just like the flowers you have seen, and the vegetables we eat."

"Can you eat a tree?" asked Zeno.

"No, it's too big, too hard, and it doesn't taste very nice . . . You can eat the leaves of some trees, though. But there are much better things to eat."

"It's not like a flower at all," said Atlanta positively. "It hasn't got any petals."

Troy pressed the control pin, and a picture of a horse-chestnut, with all its crimson 'candles' in full bloom, came on to the screen. "There's a tree that is full of flowers. Aren't they lovely?"

"They ought to be in a hydroponics tank," said Atlanta with conviction, "where they could have plenty of nitrates and phosphates."

"Trees take all they want from the soil," explained Troy.

"Why don't we have soil on *Solarian*, then?" asked Zeno excitedly. "I could grow a tree and be like the king."

"Like what king?" Troy knew there would be a logical connection somewhere.

"King Charles," announced Zeno triumphantly. "It says in

the story-film that he climbed in an oak tree to escape . . . Do you think he wore a pressure suit?"

"No. I've told you dozens of times that the Earth was surrounded by air. He could breathe just as well as we can inside the ship."

"He couldn't," said Zeno.

"Why not?"

"Cos the air was poisoned. That's why he couldn't. Cos the poison made everything die . . . He must have worn a pressure suit!"

Troy suppressed her irritation. "The air wasn't poisoned until four hundred years after King Charles was dead."

"I don't want to look at trees," said Atlanta. "Let's have that picture of the black pussy-cat again."

In spite of the controlled cabin temperature, and the warm white blanket on which she was lying, Roma felt curiously cold. It was a coldness that began inside, began in the pit of her stomach and wormed its way stealthily through the rational defences of the mind.

She stared at her own pale flesh, at the breasts that were still almost as compact and firm as before the birth of her child, at the gentle curve of her abdomen and the smooth muscular line of her thighs. She looked at her body as if it were no longer to be trusted, as if it had become her enemy.

Jung followed her gaze, sensing the conflict of emotions, the fears that hammered against the citadel of her personality; the disappointment of the unborn . . .

Suddenly, she sat up and turned towards him, trying to interpret the message in his eyes.

"What's the verdict?" Her words came slowly, reluctantly.

"No more babies, I am afraid. That is definite."

"Is that all? I mean, there's no need to hold anything back. I shan't throw hysterics."

"I shall need to operate."

"When?"

"Whenever you are ready."

She was silent for a moment, gathering her resources.

"I don't suppose there is any possible doubt?"

"None whatever. It is cancer of the uterine cervix."

"Wouldn't it be possible to use radio-tantalum, or cobalt?"

Jung did not answer immediately.

At length, he said: "Surgery is the most effective method—

in this case . . . Of course, tantalum would retard the advance, but not sufficiently to make it worth while. You see, star-flight seems to accelerate the process once it starts."

"Is that why you did not use radiotherapy on Athene's breast?"

"Yes."

"Two women out of five," said Roma, "in the first five years. It's a grim proportion."

"Athene will still bear children," he reminded her.

"Even so, at such a rate the life-unit becomes endangered. I wonder if the star-children will develop more resistance?"

"It seems probable."

"Why do you say that?"

"Because already they are able to stand more radiation than any of us."

Roma swung down from the bench and began to dress herself. "I think I would prefer hypnosis . . . It would be better than anesthetics, wouldn't it—from your point of view?"

"Undoubtedly."

There was something in his manner that troubled her. He seemed unusually reticent, almost remote. Perhaps it was only that he felt his responsibility. Or perhaps it was something more . . .

"Don't you think you ought to tell me?" she said quietly.

Jung looked startled for a moment, then he recovered himself. "Tell you what?" he parried.

"The rest."

Looking into his eyes, she was aware of a strange impersonal tenderness. It made her oddly afraid.

"I don't know that there is any more to tell." The words came smoothly, but his voice was uncertain.

"Oh yes, you do . . . You may be a good psychiatrist and a fine surgeon, but you are not a very efficient liar."

"It is just that I'm a little out of practice."

Impulsively, Roma took his hand, lifted it and studied the sensitive fingers. "They are skilled enough to cut away unhealthy tissue," she said, in a voice that could only just be heard, "but not to cut out uncertainty . . . Please don't hide anything. I want the truth—all of it."

His fingers tightened round hers. "Thousands of surgeons have faced this problem," he said, "and none of them have ever discovered what the right answer is . . . You see, my dear, it is not a question of physical pain."

She nodded, surprised at her own calmness. "How long can you give me?"

"Alpha Centauri is three light-years away," he said. "Probably, we shall not find hospitable planets, and the *Solarian* will have to voyage for another thirty years or so before we can try the next star . . . Personally, I think none of the first generation will ever set foot on a planet again."

"I understand," she answered. "I am not to delude myself that I shall be present when we reach Alpha Centauri . . . But you are being evasive. How many years?"

"If you will let me do all I can," said Jung carefully, "there may be five—that are worth having."

"I see . . . Thank you . . . When—when it becomes difficult, you will know what to do for me, won't you?"

"I will."

The color was returning to her face, and she had begun to smile. "Take care of your fingers," she said, half joking. "Because they have suddenly become very important."

As she turned towards the door, Jung said: "I would like you to remember something."

She looked at him expectantly.

"I would like you to remember," he said, "that it may be better to journey than to arrive."

Athene had just checked the first re-cycling unit in the hydro-lab, and was carefully replenishing the solution in the shallow glass reservoirs. With the exceptions of the store-chambers and power unit, the hydro-lab was the largest single department in the *Solarian*; for it contained a battery of hydroponics tanks, the whole of the re-cycling apparatus, and a laboratory which, though small, fulfilled its purpose admirably.

Being absorbed in her task, Athene did not notice Rilke's presence until he spoke to her.

"Having fun with the bacteria?"

She looked up, shook her dark curly hair and smiled. "The D.I. culture, as always, is slightly unpredictable; but I still have the little devils under control—I hope."

"If they need any disciplinary action," returned Rilke flippantly, "don't forget to call in the big bad biologist."

"I won't . . . How is Alexandria getting along? I haven't seen much of her lately."

"Need you ask?" said Rilke drily. "We are all one big happy family. Everyone is so nice and understanding, and we all help each other. The *Solarian* is a hygienic little Utopia—in a nutshell . . . It's so boring I'm often tempted to take a long walk into space."

"Don't be so bitter. You knew what it would be like before—"

"Fair warning, Athene," he cut in. "If you are going to remind me of our duty to the species, our starry destiny and all that nonsense, I'll hit you with a cylinder of oxygen . . . Newton provides quite enough propaganda himself, without anyone taking up the refrain."

"If you are feeling bad-tempered, you ought to walk it off on the hull."

"I'm not feeling bad-tempered, I'm feeling . . ." He tailed away lamely.

"What?" Athene gave him a look of cool detachment.

"You know damned well!"

"Perhaps . . . But the confirmation might be interesting."

Rilke looked at her uncertainly, wondering if she was laughing at him. "I'm in love with you," he said suddenly.

"I thought you were," was the calm reply. But her eyes softened.

"What are we going to do about it?"

She did not answer.

He asked again, gripping her shoulders, forcing a reaction.

"Nothing," said Athene.

"I thought I might mean something to you."

"Perhaps you do."

"Then?" His eyes demanded a response, an acceptance.

"Nothing at all," she repeated, but her voice was less certain.

"We'll see about that," said Rilke, tightening his grip.

"Look at it from the biological angle," she pleaded.

He grinned. "I'd love to!"

Athene's color deepened. "Don't be an idiot! You know what I mean . . . We have to regard the *Solarian* as a sort of controlled experiment."

"With five pairs of white mice," he added ironically.

"Exactly!" Her reply was vehement. "And I am not going to allow either myself or you to make it more complicated. We have enough on our hands without indulging in variations on a sexual theme."

"That's what you think!"

He slipped his other arm round her shoulders. Immediately, Athene tried to break away, but her efforts lacked conviction. Presently, the value of controlled experiments began to seem less important.

"How interesting!" The voice was at once quiet and scathing. "What's this—a biodynamic survey, or the Rape of Lucrece?"

Rilke swung round quickly. Athene stifled an exclamation.

From the mid-entrance of the hydro-lab, Socrates walked towards them.

"Hell," said Lavoisier irritably. "If you let that child come near my log-book again, I'll brain it."

He and Troy were in their private cabin. The child, Atlanta, clung to her mother tearfully.

"Do you realize what it is, trying to bring up children in a—a tin cylinder?" she demanded with anger.

"I realize that our sweet child nearly destroyed a month's work."

"You should have microfilmed it," accused Troy. "In any case, why this breathtaking urgency? We have precious little to do, and twenty years in which to do it." Suddenly, she giggled.

"What's there to laugh at?" he asked truculently.

Troy threw a significant glance at Atlanta. "It has just occurred to me that there might be someone to call you grandpa by then."

Lavoisier's irritation subsided as quickly as it had risen. "Do you regret making the star-voyage, Troy—with me?"

"Especially not, with you."

"In spite of the fact that I'm often bad-tempered?"

Troy smiled. "It's better than boredom—or indifference."

"Don't you ever regret leaving Europe Three?"

"What a question! Sometimes, I have a desperate desire to see streets and houses again, and different faces, and sunlight, and crops on the living soil . . . When you were a child, did you ever cry for the moon?"

"I don't think so."

"Well, I did . . . Now and again, I still feel like a child, and then I cry for the Earth . . . It's so long ago, it seems like a dream."

"A dream that was once lovely and terrible," added Lavoisier with unusual eloquence. "I know how you feel. One can go on for days without giving it any thought, then suddenly there is a sharp stab of nostalgia. I even get nostalgic for that wretched plastic dome!"

"Daddy," said Atlanta, choosing her moment with precocious cunning, "please tell me the Story of the Farm."

"What, again? You must have heard it hundreds of times."

"Yes, please. I want all about the pigs and the hens and the cows and the horses, and everything."

"You had better sit on my knee, then . . . That's better. Now, once upon a time . . ."

Almost directly astern of the *Solarian* was a bright star: almost directly ahead was another. Between the two, there seemed to be a taut invisible wire along which the starship hurtled at a velocity that would have seemed preposterous to the men who built her. Yet, in the vastness of interstellar journeys, a speed that might be measured in thousands of miles per second was almost meaningless—a mere loitering in the alleyways of darkness, a snail's pace through the arid desert of light-years.

To the woman who stood alone on the *Solarian's* hull, gazing first at the star ahead, then at the one astern, space and time were concepts that did not fall very clearly within the borders of reality. Space and time had become no more than a pattern of darkness, stitched together by unwinking stars.

Vienne had long since formed the habit of occasionally walking on the hull by herself. Even in her pressure suit, when she looked out, it was possible to imagine that she was alone in the fields of Earth on some unimaginably clear winter evening, reading the dusty message of the stars.

Listening carefully, she would pretend to hear the distant murmur of cities, the nearer sounds of dogs and cats and night-birds, the rustling of trees, the low voice of the wind.

It was an illusion of pain and beauty, a memorial for things that were slipping into the vague confusing pit of memory; the silent swan song of a world that had gone for ever.

Now, the only real world was a metal cylinder, a life-capsule; a tribe of ten adults and seven infants who endured the routine of prisoners, and whose only secret was hope.

Now, the real world was itself a synthetic, finite universe.

A slowly falling seed.

Chapter Four

The Tenth Year

Extract from the registers of the *Solarian*:

Individual	*Sex*	*Date of Birth (Star Time)*	*Parents*
Atlanta	F	27-9-01	Lavoisier: Troy
Zeno	M	15-11-01	Jung: Vienne
Unnamed (Mongol)	M	23-12-01	Rilke: Alexandria
Verona	F	10-3-02	Newton: Roma
Faraday	M	17-7-02	Socrates: Athene
Shannon	F	22-4-03	Rilke: Alexandria
Unnamed (atavism)	M	23-1-04	Jung: Vienne
Montaigne	M	9-5-04	Lavoisier: Troy
Carmel	F	18-11-05	Socrates: Athene
Lucerne	F	3-3-06	Jung: Vienne
Leonardo	M	22-11-06	Lavoisier: Troy
Unnamed (malform)	M	5-7-07	Socrates: Athene
Mozart	M	13-10-08	Lavoisier: Troy
Corunna	F	24-11-09	Socrates: Athene

Individual	*Sex*	*Age*	*Date of Death (Star Time)*	*Cause —Remarks*
Unnamed (Mongoloid type)	M	1 day	24-12-01	Euthanasia
Unnamed (Microcephalic)	M	1 day	24-1-04	Euthanasia
Rilke	M	34 yrs	17-7-06	Explosive decompression: Open Verdict
Unnamed (Malformation heart and eyes)	M	1 day	6-7-07	Euthanasia
Roma	F	34 yrs	14-9-09	Euthanasia disseminant cancer

Alexandria was in the library using a microbook viewer. For the last three years, she had been studying biology intensively under the guidance of Jung and Lavoisier, so that the gap created by Rilke's unexplained death would not be permanent. For it was essential that the life-unit should maintain, in spite of personal loss, its collective knowledge. Also—as far as Alexandria was concerned—it was a way of fighting back against boredom and frustration.

The question of polygamy had been raised in Council from time to time; but no one had been particularly enthusiastic—least of all, Alexandria. The rewards it offered were few, and the problems numerous. The dangers of inbreeding, on a voyage that might last for several generations, already constituted a serious hazard, which polygamy would only serve to accelerate. And, as Jung pointed out, the psychological barriers formed by people who had grown up in a monogamous culture could not be disturbed without serious risk and unforeseen consequences.

So Alexandria accepted her lonely role, drawing what consolation she might from Shannon, her daughter, now a healthy, precocious seven year old.

The years of star-flight had produced different effects on different members of the life-unit. Some began to show their age, and the effects of limited exercise and artificial sunlight. Some had lines of responsibility and tension engraved on their foreheads; but one or two seemed almost as young as they were when the star-flight began.

Strangely enough, Alexandria, though she had lost her first child and had later faced the death of Rilke, seemed least affected by personal tragedy or the monotony of the voyage. Being a naturally demonstrative and emotional person, she had expressed her feelings freely, instead of allowing them to turn inward and slowly smoulder. Now, at thirty-three, and looking seven or eight years younger, she unconsciously emphasized her position as the youngest member of the first generation. At times, even, she seemed nearer to the second generation than the first.

Not so with Newton. At thirty-nine, he looked six years older—and tired. In all the affairs of the life-unit, his was the final responsibility, the final decision. From euthanasia to acceleration programs, from social disputes to educational gradings, he was the high judge and final court of appeal. Few of his problems had been easy: many had been appalling. And then there had been the affair of Roma—the last months of inarticulate tenderness, of increasing love and forced nonchalance. And finally, as the cancer continued its implacable advance, the fixing of a date for euthanasia —which not even Roma would know, so that she might break off the star-journey while still remaining personally serene . . . That had been a secret shared only by Newton and Jung . . .

Without hearing anything, without looking up, Alexandria knew that someone else had just entered the library. She knew also that it was Newton.

"Am I disturbing you?"

She stepped back from the microbook viewer and smiled. "It is nice to be disturbed once in a while . . . Are you doing the Grand Tour?"

"No, I finished the inspection a few hours ago. As a matter of fact, I wanted to talk to you."

"Why didn't you call me over the intercom?"

Newton gave her a rueful grin. "It seemed to be a case where I ought to come to you."

"Now I am really in a panic," said Alexandria slyly. "Have I muddled up the lists, or something?" There was a quiet amusement in her eyes.

"This is going to be more difficult than I thought," he confessed. "I had it all planned out what I was going to say. But the plan seems to have collapsed."

"Don't make me lose faith in your omniscience."

"Why shouldn't I?" he smiled. "I haven't much faith in it myself."

Alexandria gazed at him speculatively: "What *do* you want to see me about?"

It was several seconds before Newton thought of what seemed to be a reasonable approach. "Do you ever think about the sort of lives we led back on Earth?" he asked abruptly.

"Often. Who doesn't?"

"Do you—do you ever regret exchanging a few months of relatively civilized existence for all these years of interstellar time?"

She didn't answer immediately.

"Not now," she admitted at length. "I used to—but it was futile, because I know really that I would have hated to stay behind."

"You're still enthusiastic about giving the human race a new start," he demanded, "even after ten years?"

Alexandria laughed. "Heavens no! The human race is only an undeveloped theory: I much prefer the simple facts."

"What are 'the simple facts'?"

"People," came the reply. "People like Vienne and Troy—and Roma . . . People like you and Jung . . . They are much more important to me than founding a new civilization or colonizing a new planetary system. I have lost my higher motives, I'm afraid. If I'm glad I made the star-voyage, it is chiefly because of one or two people who are making it with me . . . My philosophy has become very simple—I just want to take happiness when and where I can find it."

Newton stared at her. "So much for the intellectuals," he laughed. "You are probably saner than all of us put together. Which makes my task a little easier."

"What task?" She pretended total ignorance.

Newton took a deep breath: "Rilke is dead, and so is Roma. We both, I think, loved them, but—"

"No," she interrupted calmly, "we'll keep the record straight. I'm afraid I didn't love Rilke."

"Fair enough," said Newton coolly, "but I *did* love Roma. Perhaps I was just lucky."

"I think you were."

He began to play absently with a coil of microfilm, then he continued without meeting her gaze: "I was trying to lead up to the fact that you and I are alone now, Alexandria. I don't think it is a good thing—apart from personal feelings . . . I want you to be my partner."

Her eyes became curiously bright. "Back on Earth," she said quietly, "in the old days, you might have said: I love you, I want to marry you."

"I might have said it," agreed Newton, "in a ballroom or on a park bench, in a busy street or the corner of a tiny garden. I might have offered you a ring, and talked of the home we would build. There might have been a church wedding and a three-decker cake . . . But now, I can only say: I want you to be my partner."

"I don't give a damn!" she announced with sudden conviction.

Newton stared wearily at the deck. "I was afraid of that—so let's consider it all unsaid . . . You see, I have hoped—"

"Stop being an idiot," said Alexandria.

Newton prepared for a disorderly retreat; but she gripped his arm, making him look at her. With a dull detachment, he wondered whether she would offer him mockery or pity.

"I meant I didn't give a damn about old-fashioned proposals and rings and three-decker cakes," she explained gently. "If you didn't know it before, you'd better realize it now: I have been in love with you a long time—nearly ten years, I think . . . As a scientist, darling, you are not a very careful observer!"

For a moment, Newton stared at her incredulously; then wondered why women usually choose the wrong time to cry.

Extract from Jung's private journal:

What is the passage of years and the routine of star-flight doing to us all? Individually, we display different symptoms: collectively, we are all undergoing the same metamorphosis. Our values and attitudes are subjected to a kind of cosmic drift. What was once important is now unimportant: what was once trivial is now momentous.

Once, the lunch-table gossip centered on the new worlds we would discover, the civilization we would raise, the fate of the Earth we have left, and the possible destinies of other starships. Now we are all concerned with the vital question of *X* being adjusted, or *Y* being frustrated, or *Z* being neurotic. Once we thought of our departure from Earth as an escape; but now we have developed the mentality of prisoners.

We have escaped into the prison of the *Solarian*, where the entire cosmos is one hundred meters long and twenty meters wide. We have established a tribe; but what are our tribal gods? They are: personality, which represents power; knowledge, which represents power; and the manifestation of that power in an unending game of psycho-politics.

For instance, no one openly questions Newton's leadership; yet Lavoisier and Socrates challenge it secretly. They feel that Newton is not sufficiently dominant (which is to their advantage) and they resent his willingness to be persuaded by reasoned argument.

Each would prefer a system of unquestioned Authority—for himself. So it becomes of paramount importance whether, in spite of Newton's calculations, we increase ship elocity by five per cent or, in face of Socrates' protests, decrease it by nine per cent. It is no longer a problem in physics: it is a trial of strength.

Socrates, in particular, must be watched carefully. He is approaching breaking point. Ever since the death of Rilke, he has displayed signs of abnormal stress. He has undergone cyclic crises of violent self-assertion in relation to Athene and the rest of the unit. He seems to have developed a private reality, a secret world in which his dictatorial impulse is partly sublimated. Eventually, it may become more real for him than the life-unit . . .

I have never been satisfied with the explanation of Rilke's death. He was alone on the hull, and his pressure suit developed a leak, causing explosive decompression. When I treated Athene for an acute anxiety neurosis, she admitted that Rilke was 'in love' with her and that Socrates knew of it. She would not, however, reveal her own attitude; and I could not force a re-orientation because she was in the seventh month with Carmel (Rilke's child?). Later she refused treatment.

When Rilke died, Socrates was the only one with a perfect alibi. He was in Newton's room, discussing a velocity equation with him—until Newton left him to make the hull inspection. It was Newton who discovered the body, and who—if it was murder and not misadventure—would fall under suspicion. But Socrates is a brilliant engineer with a penchant for complex time mechanisms . . .

Socrates has displayed many signs of paraphrenia—which would certainly make him quite capable of murder. But assuming that he was guilty, what could be done about it?

For all normal purposes, the affair is now history. In any case, on the *Solarian* we cannot afford the luxury of vengeance: we can only take precautions.

Obviously, his tension must be dealt with in some way. He must be driven out of his regression . . . Hypno-analysis, perhaps? He would need to be completely off-guard—which is a difficult proposition . . .

Such, now are the major problems in our tiny capsule of life. If we or our descendants manage to found a second human civilization, this journal may perhaps find a place in the archives . . . I wonder if it will convey to you, the historians of the future, something of our mood—the constricted atmosphere of our journey through the long years of star-travel?

The schoolroom was a scene of intense creative activity. Zeno, Atlanta, Faraday and Verona were engaged in modelling in soft plastics, while the younger ones were kept out of mischief by a tri-di fairy story which was projected for them on a small corner screen.

Faraday laid down his palette knife with a triumphant air: "What do you think of that?" His plastic mammoth, though only a few inches high, had excellent proportions. Faraday, with an eye for detail, had managed to give its hide a textural roughness.

The other children gazed at it critically.

"A silly old elephant," said Atlanta contemptuously.

"It's not an elephant, it's a mammoth."

"A silly old mammoth, then. That's not very exciting at all."

"It's a million years old," protested Faraday, trying to justify himself. "It used to kill people and push trees over."

"A tractor could have done that," said Zeno. "I've modelled a tractor—with electronic controls. It could have ploughed by itself without any technician . . . Tractors were more important than mammoths."

"What does 'ploughed' mean?" asked Verona.

"It means turning the soil over," explained Zeno. "The Earth-people used to do that in the days when they grew food."

Faraday studied the tractor that rivalled his mammoth anxiously. A sudden smile came over his face. "That couldn't have ploughed anything," he announced positively.

"Why not?" demanded Zeno.

"You forgot to make the ploughshares."

Zeno reddened. "No, I didn't. It's just that I'd used up all my plastic—nearly all of it, anyway."

"Tractors and mammoths!" exclaimed Atlanta. "Can't you find anything more interesting to model?"

"Let's see what *you've* done," said Zeno. He went to her modelling tray. "A house," he murmured with disgust. "What did you want to make a house for? Houses don't *do* anything."

Atlanta gazed at him belligerently. "Houses were the most important things of all," she said with conviction. "People lived in them, and they had windows that looked out on to gardens and streets. They had doors and fires, and the smoke went up a chimney . . . Look, I've made a door that really opens."

"It isn't bad," said Faraday carefully. "I mean, for a girl."

Zeno tried to change the conversation. "I know how to do Pythagoras by trigonometry. I bet no one else does."

Faraday said: "That's easy: it's the sines of two angles times the hypotenuse . . . I can use cosines, too."

"Who taught you?"

"Socrates."

"He shouldn't have done. You're not old enough."

"Oh, yes he should! I'm only eight months younger than you. He has shown me how to make electromagnets and a step-up transformer . . . I bet Jung hasn't taught you anything like that."

Zeno thought hard. "Do you know what an anxiety neurosis is?" he asked confidently.

"No, I don't—and neither do you."

"Oh, yes I do," said Zeno.

"If we are going to be clever," remarked Atlanta coldly, "I know something neither of you know. I know how to synthesize proteins."

Before either of the boys could think of a face-saving answer, Verona seized her opportunity: "No one has looked at my model yet. It's not fair."

"We will now," said Zeno quickly. The little group moved across to her tray.

Verona's piece of plastic had been moulded into a smooth oval shape with irregular lobes. The children regarded it silently for two or three seconds, trying to decide what it might be. They met with no success.

"It isn't anything at all," said Atlanta. "It's just a lump."

Verona shook her head indignantly. "It's the most lovely thing I know."

"What is it, then?" asked Zeno.

"It's a cloud," she said, "a flying cloud—filled full of wonderful rain!"

Decoded extracts from Socrates' diary:

18-7-06. One eliminated successfully. Not because of Athene, but because Rilke was weak. The evolutionary principle must be maintained. Newton is afraid of his power and afraid of losing it. That is weakness.

7-8-06. They suspect Newton, but they know he has no guts. So they call it an accident. Athene is afraid. By God, if I thought that child was Rilke's . . .

17-4-07. Jung is waiting for me. He can wait a little longer. Plenty of time.

23-9-07. Newton still won't accelerate. He wants me to make a mistake. They are all watching me. Let them.

15-1-08. If Lavoisier talks to me like that again, I'll break him in two. He's afraid of me. He knows I am going to be leader. He had better watch out.

16-3-09. Somebody changed the gas cylinder on my pressure suit. Thought they would let me jet out into space as usual, then not have enough to get back. Did they think I wouldn't check? If it's Athene, the bitch, I'll make her wish she had never been born.

3-11-09. Newton squashed my acceleration program. Only a little longer, and I'll fix that bastard for good. He let Roma go on too long. She should have had euthanasia a year ago. He hadn't the guts to do it.

5-12-09. Why does Jung give me that I'm-watching-from-afar smile of his? If he wants trouble, he can have it. Eventually, a straight fight between me and Lavoisier. At least, he's no fool.

15-12-09. Dreamt somebody was trying to strangle me while I was sleeping. Too damn real for comfort. Too many dreams lately. Wonder why? Must ask Jung for pills. No! I'll get my own pills.

23-12-09. Dreams getting worse—still the same pattern. Man with metal fingers follows me everywhere, watching what I do. When I look round, he's not there. Just see fingertips disappearing. Like knives. They are stained . . . He's waiting for me, waiting till I get to sleep. Then the fingers . . . This damned star-flight! Why does it give a man such persistent dreams?

Jung had formed a habit of spending odd half-hours on the navigation deck. It was the one place in the *Solarian* where he could be reasonably sure of solitude. Newton, of course, made routine visits, but only once every two or three days. There was, after all, no need to navigate: the ship was falling smoothly and uneventfully towards its distant target.

For Jung, the navigation deck was a link with Europe Three. He would recall, looking at the semi-circle of contour-berths, a vivid picture of firing point and the slightly unreal days that preceded it. He would remember the last days of the city, the tension, the impending violence. He would see again the anxious expressions of ten familiar strangers, waiting for the moment that would shoot them out through the plastic dome towards the stars.

Then he would turn out the light, and stare through the invisible plastiglass at the hard foam of darkness, the barely changing pattern of distant suns. Habitually, fruitlessly, he would try to extrapolate the future from the past, knowing all the time that the future was already a part of the total history, and the past was as if it might never have been . . .

This time, the light was already cut off when he got there. A sixth sense warned him of someone else's presence; warned him of danger. But, after a moment's hesitation, he went in. He found his way across to the astrodome and stood there, looking out; and listening.

He thought he heard a deep, irregular breathing somewhere. He decided to wait, knowing he would hear footsteps. He waited about three minutes, and heard the breathing steady down until it was no longer audible. *Danger,* whispered his instinct. *Don't go to the switch,* warned his intellect.

Jung was wrong about the footsteps. He did not hear any. He was aware only of a glancing blow on the shoulder. It had been destined for his head, and was heavy enough to drop him to the deck. As he fell, his assailant came on top of him—hands searching for his throat. Jung gripped a wrist, tried to twist it back; he couldn't, but he held on to it grimly.

"Did you get tired of waiting, Socrates?" he panted.

"You bloody witch-doctor! You've been eating away at my nerves, cutting off my sleep . . . But tonight . . . Tonight I sleep sound!"

In the darkness, they rolled heavily into a contour-berth. An elbow dug painfully into Jung's neck. He grabbed a handful of hair and wrenched it back.

"At least, you were more subtle with Rilke!"

"You are the man with steel fingers," grated Socrates. "I'm going to strangle you like you've tried to strangle me, you bastard!"

A sudden jerk, and Jung broke away. He groped to his feet cautiously. He heard Socrates bump into a contour-berth and curse.

"Where the hell are you?" he raged. "I'm going to tear out your guts and re-cycle you . . . No more bad dreams . . . Thus saith the Lord: I will devour mine enemies."

"Why," panted Jung, backing away, "why am I the man with steel fingers?"

"You're watching me while I work, then when I turn round you are not there. All I can see are the fingers, coming and going, waiting until I'm asleep . . . Steel fingers, trying to pulp my throat."

Associated ideas stampeded through Jung's mind. *Steel fingers; pincers; callipers; engineering; precision . . . Socrates!*

"I'm not the man with steel fingers. I'm—"

"Now I know where you are! You are blocking out patterns of stars. I can't see you, but I can see that damned smile . . . I'm going to ram your blasted fingers down your throat!"

"We are not alone, Socrates." As Jung spoke, he doubled up and tiptoed silently across the deck.

"Think I'm falling for that? No, you can't get the switch, I've shorted it. You can't get out, either—I've fixed that, too."

While he was talking and blundering towards the astrodome, Jung circled up behind him. "Someone's here," he whispered. "He's watching us." He backed away as Socrates whirled round.

"Stay still, you bastard!"

"He's watching us, Socrates."

"Like hell!" There was a savage laugh. "Now you can't get away. You are between me and the observation panels."

"He's watching us, Socrates . . . Watching us—waiting to see who wins."

Socrates hesitated. "If this is your idea of—"

"He's right by my side. Like me, he is blocking out a pattern of stars . . . Can't you see?"

Socrates stopped, shut his eyes tight, rubbed them, opened them and peered through a darkness that was now dancing with faint nebulous whirls of light.

"God Almighty! I can see him now. He's there—*shimmering!* And those long shining fingers!" The last words came in a hoarse whisper.

"He's watching you, Socrates. Watching and smiling."

"Jung, where are you? For God's sake don't leave me!"

"I'm nowhere, Socrates, nowhere at all. There are only you and him now."

"Turn on the light! For pity's sake, *turn on the light!*"

"There is no light. Only you and him."

"Don't leave me!"

"Only you and him." As he spoke, Jung began to walk slowly round, coming up once more behind Socrates, who stared transfixed at the observation panels.

"Who is he? *God, who is he?*" The words tailed into a moan.

"Don't you know?" whispered Jung. "The man with steel fingers."

"What . . . what . . . *what does he want?*"

"To kill you."

"No!"

"He wants you to die."

"No!"

"He wants to bury his steel fingers in your throat. He wants to dig down and down, until he reaches your soul. He wants to rip it with his steel fingers, so that you will never feel anything again."

"God help me!" screamed Socrates. *"What can I do?"*

"Destroy him! See how he smiles . . . You must destroy him." Jung's voice was barely a whisper.

"I can't . . . I can't do it!"

"You must."

"I can't!"

"It is him or you . . . Look at the fingers . . . See, they are reaching out."

"Who is he? Who is he?" The scream broke down into a sob.

"You know who he is."

"I don't. I can't."

"Look at him. Whose face is it?"

"Nobody's."

"Look again—before it is too late."

"Not that! It can't be!" whimpered Socrates.

"It is! The face of the man who killed Rilke. The face of violence . . . Look well, Socrates. Violence has steel fingers, but he has no eyes. The man who killed Rilke was blind, but *you* can see."

"I can't breathe," moaned Socrates.

"You must look."

"I . . . can't . . . breathe."

"What can you see?"

"Nothing . . . Nothing."

"Yes, you can. What is it?"

"A . . . a dead man. No he's not dead! He's . . . he's coming back to life. WHO IS HE?" The last three words were hammered out at the limit of endurance.

Jung reached out in the darkness to the swaying body. "His name? His name is—Socrates . . . Now you can rest."

He crumpled, and Jung lowered him gently to the deck. There he lay, breathing normally, sleeping—curled up like a tired child.

Extract from Newton's star-log:

13-12-10. Distance covered: 2.735 light-years. Unit continues to function efficiently. Second generation now well established. There have been no major crises.

We shall now be able to make fractional percentage velocity increases regularly—due to perfected nucleonic ripple-meter designed by Socrates. The voyage may be shortened by five years.

Chapter Five

The Fiftieth Year

The journey to Alpha Centauri took nineteen and a half years—nineteen and a half years of hope and resignation; of imprisonment and happiness; of love and resentment; of birth and death.

In the smooth silence of increasingly meaningless velocities, the *Solarian* had carried its tiny cargo of life towards an alien sun. And as the years went by, as the children grew up and the first generation slipped quietly into middle age, tension mounted. It became an article of faith that there *must* be a planetary system, that such a star as Alpha Centauri could not be sterile.

The children, lost in the horizons of adolescence, of sexual awakening and approaching maturity, were full of confidence; full of the theoretical lore of pioneering; full of a desire to challenge the legendary elements of wind and rain, rock and soil.

The first generation balanced precariously on a tightrope between emotional hope and intellectual despair; between intellectual optimism and emotional apathy.

While the *Solarian* was still half a light-year from its destination, Athene died. She did not die because of a disease or an accident; she did not commit suicide, nor was she killed. She died simply because there was no more stamina left. She died because she had endured much and had complained little; because her children were growing up, and Socrates no longer needed her. And then there was the memory of Rilke . . .

Socrates, who had once taken a life and afterwards faced the ordeal of putting together the fragments of his own, survived her by three months. But the second wave of that old, inescapable guilt proved too much for him. He took a pressure suit, went out on to the hull and calmly jetted into space, away from the *Solarian*, until his gas cylinders were empty. Then he opened the pressure valve.

It was Lavoisier who went out and brought his body back—not in triumph or sentimentality, but in the knowledge that the life-unit could not afford to waste any biological material at all.

Faraday, then seventeen, undertook his father's duties with the help of Newton; while Atlanta, nearly nineteen, took Athene's place without any help at all.

Occasionally, Newton would come and watch the two youngsters while they were working. He would talk to them gravely as to equals, giving them a sense of responsibility, a desire to improve their techniques, to widen their knowledge.

Seeing their youthful energy and confidence, he would be filled with silent wonder at the quality of these star-children, to whom Earth was a documented legend, and for whom the possibility of planets round Alpha Centauri was a fundamental vision of paradise.

Time wore on, and the star ahead became brighter, easily dominating the sky, visible now as a binary system to the naked eye. Four and a quarter light-years astern was another star, called Sol. A star of the first magnitude . . . A star of memory . . .

Being the astro-physicist, it was Newton who first discovered the simple, heart-breaking fact. For an agonizing week, he kept the knowledge to himself, wanting irrationally to delay the inevitable reaction until the last possible moment.

Awake, he became taciturn, preoccupied, doing what he could to tone down the general fever of expectancy. But while he was asleep, the torrent of words he had held back was released; his hidden fears were enacted in the half-reality of dreams.

Lying by his side, restless, watching him, Alexandria learned the truth. It was the first time she had ever seen Newton near to breakdown—the first time she had ever seen tears force their way from the eyes of a sleeping man.

Gently, she awakened him, offering the only possible consolation—a love that had endured for nearly nineteen years.

There was no planetary system round Alpha Centauri: the binaries were sterile.

When Newton told the life-unit, there was a sudden terrible silence. The six remaining members of the first generation stared at the bulkhead, the deck, the table—anywhere but at each other; for each was afraid of reading the message in someone else's eyes. Each was afraid of being the first to break. They sat there, waiting for the inevitable question.

"Now we shall have to change course," said Newton, endeavoring to keep his voice matter-of-fact. "Are we all still agreed on the second objective?" He glanced round anxiously at the tired and depressed faces.

"You think Sirius is our best target?" asked Jung.

"I do . . . There is even a possibility in the Companion."

His answer was received in another painful silence.

At length, Lavoisier pulled himself together. "How long?" he asked with a grim smile.

"Twenty-eight years—on the new acceleration program . . We might reduce it, of course. Obviously, that is the first problem to work on."

"You'll have to knock the guts out of neo-relativity," commented Lavoisier drily.

Again there was silence.

Then Jung made an effort to break the leaden atmosphere of futility. "Just in case anyone feels his psyche needs renovating," he said lightly, "I hereby give notice that I shall be fully occupied for the next five years—fixing up my own."

Troy suddenly began to laugh, and could not stop.

Six months later, the wide power curve was completed. Taking advantage of its space-warp, the *Solarian* swung round Alpha Centauri, picked up an extra point-seven per cent velocity, and began the long fall to Sirius.

The disappointment had been altogether less searing for the star-children. For them it was more of an intellectual disappointment; the failure of an abstract promise; the loss of an adventure. For their elders, it had been a direct assault on the citadel of hope, a time when hazy memories of planetary existence had been resurrected once more in sharp and painful clarity.

One by one, as the years went by, the children came to maturity. Slowly, they took over the running of the starship; and they began to co-operate in advanced research. Slowly, in fact and theory, they began to outstrip the first generation, whose final superiority lay only in their experience of planetary life.

One day, Atlanta and Zeno announced that they had decided to become permanent partners; and in the third year of the Sirius voyage, their first child was born. They called him Balzac.

Then Verona partnered with Montaigne; and Faraday with Shannon. Presently, the first generation, weakening under the imperceptible advance of age, found new enthusiasms in the novelty of grandchildren; and philosophically accepted their diminishing lead, their almost passive role as Elders.

Before they were halfway to Sirius, Lavoisier, who in spite of gray hair and a discreet corpulence had preserved much of his youthful vigor, suddenly began to lose strength. Zeno, now a skilled physician and surgeon, could find no organic failure. But Lavoisier continued to weaken. On the ninth day of his mysterious illness, the lower part of his body was paralysed. On the thirteenth day, he administered his own euthanasia.

Zeno performed an autopsy before the body was re-cycled. But the autopsy could not reveal the supreme weariness caused by thirty years of sustaining an unfulfilled hope. Zeno remained puzzled; but Jung knew why Lavoisier had died, and preferred to keep the knowledge to himself.

Within six months, Troy had followed her partner. Again the autopsy did not reveal any physical damage to the heart . . .

In the sixteenth year of the Sirius journey, the second generation's gradual take-over was completed by Newton's surrendering the leadership of the life-unit to Faraday, now a mathematician and physicist whose abilities exceeded those of his teacher. For Newton and the three other survivors of the first generation—Alexandria, Jung and Vienne—it was a symbolic climax. It was the handing on of a torch.

Meanwhile, the *Solarian* plunged on through the everlasting darkness. The star ahead grew steadily brighter; while Alpha Centauri, far astern, gently waned . . . Somewhere on the port quarter was a star called Sol—one of the dozen brightest. There came a time when it took even Newton a few seconds to pick it out . . .

At sixty-two, after nearly forty years of star-flight, Alexandria was still a graceful and slender woman. Her face was young and her movements firm; but a shock of snow-white hair, and a complexion that remained obstinately pallid in spite of radiation baths, proclaimed her testament of endurance.

For her, Sirius was a dream that would never come true—a myth that was valid only because it sustained the energies and ambitions of men like Faraday, Zeno and Montaigne; which, in turn, gave hope to the women and daydreams to the children; even as Alpha Centauri had once challenged and stimulated the first generation.

Alexandria, free now from the tantalizing mirage of habitable planets, concentrated on the two most important things in the entire cosmos: Newton and the grandchildren.

Newton would soon be seventy, but since he had surrendered responsibility for the *Solarian*, since he had complete confidence in Faraday's ability, a final burst of intellectual and spiritual energy generated within him. He spent his days playing chess with Jung, or argued about the meaning of life, the probable birth and death cycles of the universe, the solution of dreams, and even the Intelligence Quotients of the third generation.

In quietly accepting the fact that he would no longer be present when the *Solarian* reached Sirius, his personality entered a sort of Indian Summer.

Jung and Vienne, each in their own way, had found a similar tranquility. They no longer looked forward to reaching Sirius themselves; but their confidence had not diminished. Even though the result was still inconclusive, Jung was profoundly thankful for the privilege of journeying in the *Solarian*.

He had witnessed a unique experiment: he had seen that human life could survive the star-voyage and renew itself; that, even under such conditions, culture need not degenerate into barbarism; and that, in fact, the frontiers of human knowledge could be extended—even in such tremendous isolation.

Vienne was only a year older than Alexandria, but the star-flight did not seem to have dealt so compassionately with her. She began to find much difficulty in sleeping, and resorted more and more to drugs.

Yet she was happy. Of late, her childhood on Earth had become vivid, possessing at times a greater degree of reality than life on the *Solarian*. She experienced once again the sounds and sights of the city, the magical aura of Europe Three, seen through the eyes of innocence.

Vienne allowed herself the luxury of slipping down into the pool of memory, knowing that it was the final luxury; that she would not have much longer to wait.

Entering the schoolroom one day, on one of her frequent visits, Alexandria found that it was occupied only by six-year-old Odessa, daughter of Shannon and Faraday.

Absorbed in building with a set of well-worn bricks, the grave fair-haired child seemed quite unaware of her presence. Alexandria quietly found a chair and settled down to wait until her granddaughter felt the need of a diversion.

As she watched the small, busy fingers arranging the bricks in some incomprehensible but doubtless significant pattern, Alexandria's mind wandered back to the time when she, too, had played with similar bricks on a hearth-rug in a warm, well-remembered room. Lost in her reverie, she was no longer aware of the child, and did not notice that Odessa had suddenly abandoned her bricks and was watching her with a rapt expression. After a time, Alexandria was brought sharply back to her surroundings by the sound of an excited, childish voice.

"Oh, it was lovely, Alexandria! Do tell me that story again—please!"

She recovered herself with a start, gazing at Odessa in surprise. "What story, my dear? What are you talking about?"

"The story you just told me. I think it was the nicest I've ever had."

Alexandria stared. "But I haven't told you any story. I have just been sitting here, Odessa, watching you play with your bricks."

"You did! You did! And it was so beautiful—just as if I were seeing it all myself . . . Who was the little girl, please?"

"What little girl?" demanded Alexandria blankly.

Odessa tossed her head with impatience. "The little girl who played with the bricks on a sort of dark green carpet . . . It had orange diamonds at the corners, didn't it? I liked that. I shall do it in my drawing book."

Alexandria's mind became curiously clear. "What did my voice sound like when I was telling the story?"

A frown came over the child's face. "I—I don't know."

"Did you see my lips moving?"

"N-no. That's why it was so nice . . . Have I done something wrong?" There was a suspicion of tears.

Alexandria made herself relax, and smiled. "No, darling.

You haven't done anything wrong at all. I am just being an old silly . . . Tell you what—wouldn't it be nice if *you* told *me* the story?"

"No, it wouldn't," retorted the child positively.

"Just this once," pleaded Alexandria. "I have something nice in my pocket . . . You can have it when you have told me."

"What is it?"

"Sugar-stick."

"All right." said Odessa reluctantly. "But you must promise to tell me another one afterwards."

"I promise."

"Without opening your lips?" insisted the child. "It's much nicer like that."

"I'll try," said Alexandria doubtfully. "Now, you tell the story back to me—right from the beginning . . . We'll pretend it's a sort of game."

The child picked herself up and calmly perched on Alexandria's knee. "Well," she began, "there was a cosy little room—just like the ones you see in picture-tales—with a big window. And you could see people walking outside, and they didn't wear pressure suits, and there were strange things with wheels that moved very quickly and made a lot of noise . . . And the little girl sat on a green rug, with orange diamonds at the corners; and she built a pile of bricks and put a little silver bell on top, and said *church* . . . What is *church*, Alexandria?"

"It's like a very big house—but please go on, darling." Alexandria stared at her, fascinated.

"Well," continued Odessa, unperturbed, "she said *church* and rang the bell. Then a big man came into the room, and the little girl laughed at him. He picked her up and lifted her right over his head, and said one day he'd take her to a big *church* and *marry* her. . . . What is *marry?*"

Alexandria was trying hard to hide her tears. "It's—it's when people become partners . . . Is that all, Odessa?"

"Yes, that's the end . . . Why are you crying? Have I made you unhappy?"

"No, darling. It was a lovely story."

Odessa smiled doubtfully. "Now tell me who the little girl was."

"It . . . it was me." The words were a hoarse whisper.

"Please, Alexandria, can I have another story? You promised . . . Without opening your lips."

"I am going away for a few minutes, darling. Then I will come back again. While I am gone, I want you to draw that story for me, and color it in . . . Then I will try to tell you another one."

"Please," said Odessa, "I'd like the sugar-stick now."

Alexandria fumbled in her pocket, produced the small sweet, then rushed blindly from the schoolroom in search of Jung.

Eventually, it was discovered that the third generation contained three natural telepaths. Odessa, Granada and Kepler. This was regarded as a development of tremendous importance. It presented new horizons, new problems, new opportunities.

During his remaining years, Jung devoted much of his time to helping the three children to co-ordinate their advancing techniques. Presently, they were able to draw clearly upon the mental experience of almost everyone on the *Solarian*. And they learned to pool their resources, to experience the thought-patterns of each other.

Because of this, their intellectual development was extraordinarily rapid. From the minds of the first generation, they took a vivid background of terrestrial existence; from the second generation they gathered the whole panorama of theoretical science; and from each other they took the final siftings of their communal harvest.

Between the three of them, this extrasensory perception was a bond that grew stronger and stronger. Soon, they no longer seemed to act as separate beings, as independent personalities: it was as if they recognized a fundamental unity, as if each acknowledged and was subject to a kind of triple personality.

No one was surprised when, ten years later, after the Sirius catastrophe, Kepler announced that he wished to be partnered with Odessa *and* Granada. It was the first case of polygamy; it was also an experiment that was too valuable to be interrupted.

For it was evident to those who survived the disaster that the next leader of the life-unit would be as far beyond Newton and Faraday as *homo sapiens* was beyond the anthropoids: the next leader would be an *over-mind*—the welding of three separate streams of consciousness, of three separate reservoirs of experience, into one para-human being.

But before Kepler, Odessa and Granada were ready to fulfil their destiny, there was the ordeal of Sirius . . .

In the twenty-fifth year of the Sirius voyage, Alexandria and Newton took euthanasia together, and enjoyed the last luxury of giving up the star-journey in each other's arms. Eight months earlier, Vienne had slipped into a final coma. Jung would still have been able to count on another year or two, but life was not so dear to him that he wished to face it without the companion who had held his affection for forty-five years.

So he said goodbye to Newton and Alexandria, gave a last injection to the small unconscious body that was all that remained of Vienne, then lay down by her side and closed his eyes peacefully.

Jung did not need to practice physical euthanasia on himself. The knowledge he had gained in his explorations of the human psyche enabled him without difficulty to release his own will to live.

For him, the star-voyage had never been a problem of light-years, of velocities and destinations; it had been a problem and an experiment in human relationships. He was satisfied, even without reaching an hospitable planet, that the problem had been solved, that the experiment was successful.

He had found that the answer lay in reversing an old religious truth. Man had created God in his own image—as an everlasting ideal; a symbol of the perfection for which he himself would always strive; a symbol of his own wonder, his own creativity, his own pursuit of love and beauty.

Jung had discovered that Man was not fundamentally good or bad—but fundamentally Godlike . . . With this knowledge, he was content to rest, knowing that the *Solarian's* destiny lay not in its destination, but in the nature of the journey . . . And the journey was good.

During the last few years with Jung and Vienne, when the four of them had drawn closer together, Alexandria and Newton had caught something of this vision; and when the time came, they also gave up the star-journey in peace and dignity. Death seemed no more than a whisper; and life, a freely surrendered fulfilment.

Also in the twenty-fifth year of the Sirius voyage was another climax—of an unusual kind. Kepler, then a serious boy of thirteen, already with half a dozen sciences at his finger-tips, came to Faraday with a peculiar warning, and with an extraordinary piece of advice:

"I hope you won't laugh at me, Faraday," he began, "but I want to tell you something that seems very important." He gazed at the assured, middle-aged man anxiously.

Faraday cocked an eyebrow. "I won't laugh . . . Now, what is it?"

Kepler shuffled his feet restlessly, and cleared his throat with a nervous cough. Finally, he plucked up courage. "I think we ought to change the Solarian's course."

"You what!" Faraday was utterly taken aback.

"I think we ought to change course. Procyon is a very good alternative, and—"

"Before we go any further," said Faraday carefully, "let me remind you that the destination was selected long before you were born. When the original calculations were made, Newton estimated the voyage at twenty-eight years, and hoped to cut even that time. He was reckoning without the space-drift, of course, which they hadn't appreciated then . . . Now under the old velocity, this trip would have taken over forty years; and even with the sub-galactic drive, we won't be there before the voyage has reached its thirtieth year . . . So if you are serious, you had better have a very sound reason."

Kepler looked crestfallen, but he was persistent. "I would not have bothered you if I hadn't thought it was—urgent."

Something in his tone made Faraday oddly afraid. "Then you'd better tell me all about it."

"As a matter of fact, you gave me the reason," said Kepler.

"I?" Faraday was astounded.

"Occasionally, I seem to become attuned to your—your precognitive memory . . . The last time it happened, about ten hours ago, I discovered that we ought not to keep on the Sirius voyage."

"Just *what* led to that discovery?" Faraday sounded ominous. He still found it difficult to get used to the fact that for telepaths not to explore the mental experience of their companions would be as frustrating as normal people going about with their eyes permanently closed.

There was a final hesitation, then Kepler took the plunge: "I learned that we should find no planets round Sirius."

"From my precognitive memory?" demanded Faraday with scepticism.

"Yes . . . I also learned that it would be dangerous to carry our investigation to the Companion of Sirius."

"No planets there, either, I suppose?" Faraday did not take the trouble to disguise his irritation.

Kepler realized that he was being made to look foolish, but he stuck to his point. "That's the danger. The Companion does have planets—a system of five."

"What a relief to know that we haven't got much further to travel," said Faraday ironically. "I don't suppose my precognitive memory was sufficiently obliging to tell you which planet would prove the most attractive?"

"I'm afraid it did—planet three . . . I know this sounds stupid, Faraday, but I had to warn you." His eyes were an eloquent appeal for Faraday to take him seriously.

"Why *warn* me? Surely if your little piece of clairvoyance is correct, we all have reason to rejoice?"

Kepler became desperate. "Don't ask me how or why, because I can't explain. But I do know that planet three of the Companion's system—if we ever investigate it—will be a terrible danger . . . I *know* that, Faraday, because unconsciously you know it."

"Unconsciously or otherwise, I seem to know the devil of a lot . . . Can you tell me exactly what this danger is?"

"No, the image isn't clear."

Faraday was silent for a moment or two; then, seeing the apprehensive look on Kepler's face, he gave him a friendly smile. "You know what I think? I think you are finding E.S.P. something of a strain. I think you are confusing telepathy with imagination."

"I swear I'm not! I tried to pretend that I was imagining the whole thing, but it wouldn't work."

"Well, then, I shall have to treat you to a little logic . . . You say you dredged this information from my precognitive memory?"

"Yes."

"You drew, not upon present supposition, but upon future fact?"

"If you want to put it like that."

"In short, you tapped a memory of *what will have happened.*"

"Yes . . . I suppose so."

"In which case," said Faraday triumphantly, "there is nothing we can do about it, is there?"

"Why?"

"Because if it is a future fact, it is inevitable; and if it is not a future fact, your argument for changing course falls to bits . . . I'm sorry, Kepler, but you seem to get the worst of it both ways."

"You are trapping me with determinism," said Kepler reproachfully.

"My dear boy, you are being trapped with common sense. If I can remember in advance that we visit planet three of the Companion, then we certainly must visit planet three—otherwise the bottom has been knocked out of precognitive memory; and we are back where we were, with absolutely no reason to change course."

"I'm sorry I troubled you . . . But if the Companion does have a system, and if planet three turns out to be the most attractive, you'll—"

Faraday grinned. "I'll make a public confession, and we'll be as cautious as the devil. That is a promise. Does it satisfy you?"

"Well . . . I still wish you would switch to Procyon."

Faraday ruffled the boy's hair affectionately. "Get out before I brain you!"

Four and a half years later, when he was nearly eighteen, Kepler had the bitter satisfaction of knowing that he had been right about Sirius; and the dissatisfaction of realizing that for the rest of the life-unit, with the exceptions of Odessa and Granada, it proved absolutely nothing. Although thirty years of hope had again foundered on the discovery of another barren star, not even the heartrending disappointment could swamp the intellectual acceptance of the odds being grimly against the formation of a planetary system.

By that time, the effect of Kepler's pessimistic warning on those members of the life-unit who took it seriously was the reverse of what he had intended. They were eager to begin the voyage to the Companion to see whether his predicted system of five planets did in fact exist.

His still repeated warnings of danger were rationalized on the grounds that if there were planets, there was bound to be danger—plenty of it—but only from the natural hazards to be encountered on any planetary investigation. And should Planet Three turn out to be the most propitious, forewarned was as good as being forearmed, and the expedition would proceed only with supreme caution

The mood of the life-unit slowly swung, pendulum-wise

back to a moderate optimism . . . Compared with the fatalistic endurance required for journeys through deep space that were measured by the light-year, the Companion voyage would be a mere hop, a matter of ten or eleven months. Another twenty-five hundred million miles of interstellar darkness, and the mystery of the Companion of Sirius would be solved.

During the wide power curve round Sirius, when the *Solarian* had actually to go further away from the Companion in order to bring it on course, Faraday seemed unusually preoccupied. Being the astro-physicist, he was already in possession of facts that would not be evident to the rest of the unit for some time—unless he chose to reveal them

He had discovered after weeks of exhausting observation that Kepler was—right. The Companion did possess planets. Faraday's careful telescopy had tracked down one, and his mathematical calculations had inferred the presence of at least another two.

As time wore on, he would gaze at Procyon with increasing frequency; and he began to wonder whether the strange results of Kepler's E.S.P. could possibly justify an abrupt diversion and a journey of at least forty years.

A decision had to be reached quickly. After fruitless hours of self-questioning, after innumerable examinations of the available data, he decided that for better or worse the Companion voyage must be continued. If the *Solarian* suddenly switched course to Procyon, all aboard—with the exception of the telepaths—would regret the lost opportunity, the tantalizing question mark they had left behind.

It was too much to ask of human beings that, after nearly fifty years of star-journey, they should refuse to explore the first system of planets that had been discovered.

As soon as he had reached the decision, Faraday's conscience made him want to explain the predicament fully to Kepler. He did not need to: Kepler explained it to him.

The eighteen year old boy gave him a rueful smile, and said calmly: "You don't need to tell me, I understand A month ago, you discovered the existence of the three inner planets; and that made you consider again whether I really was being just—just imaginative . . Since then, you have been thinking it over quietly, and you have decided that we can't throw away the opportunity to explore—even though precognitive memory seems to have its points . . . Isn't that right?"

"Well, I'll be damned! Have you told anyone?"

"I haven't *told* anyone, but Odessa and Granada already know."

"I see . . . I suppose there's no reason why we should keep it a secret any longer . . . I give you my word we'll take the utmost precautions."

"I was afraid you would," said Kepler enigmatically.

Faraday threw him a questioning glance. "Has my unconscious memory pattern provided you with any more revelations?" he asked casually.

Kepler's expression was somber. "No. It is as if a barrier has been set up, and I can't break through."

Planet One was hardly more than a fragment of cosmic ash, too near its parent sun to have ever supported life; Planet Two was also desolate, a barren wilderness in a shroud of eternal steam; Planet Four was a red desert whose contours were changed rapidly by an apparently unending sequence of tornadoes; Planet Five was an icy waste, far beyond the Companion's operative field of radiant heat.

There remained Planet Three.

Its diameter was a little more than two thousand miles; but of all the Companion's system, it was clearly the most promising. By terrestrial standards, it was a rocky ball of tundra, with only a thin green belt in the equatorial region.

But to the inhabitants of the *Solarian*, whose knowledge of Earth was drawn only from histographical films and microrecords, it seemed a veritable paradise. Even the atmosphere was convenient, being a sixty-five/thirty-five mixture of helium and oxygen. It began to seem possible that *homo sapiens* might establish a flourishing colony on Planet Three.

After a preliminary survey, the starship went into orbit at an altitude of five hundred miles, so that surface conditions could be studied carefully. Three days later, the altitude was reduced to two hundred and fifty miles; and after a further three days of careful observation, the decision was taken to go down.

In a fever of expectancy and hope, the life-unit prepared to explore. It was conceded, of course, that Kepler had been right, and that a certain amount of danger would be inevitably attendant upon the unit's first planetary exploration.

But, with that tempting surface stretched like a map below, it was also agreed that the danger had probably been overemphasized, and that precognitive memory patterns were not likely to be as accurate as scientific instruments. The collective conscience was satisfied by a resolution to proceed with extreme caution.

The touch-down, achieved without any difficulty on one of the smooth equatorial plains, was a moment of supreme emotion for the impatient prisoners. As the four landing supports bit firmly into the surface, the volatility rockets died, and there was silence—the silence of arrival, the end of a long darkness.

The surface temperature was equable, with no greater variation than that of a mild European summer. The vegetation was confined to moss, lichen and fern, and other simple cryptogams. The animal life was restricted to tiny, undeveloped insects.

There was no warning of the disaster; nor, afterwards, was there any evidence of its nature.

But on the fifth day, Verona complained of a slight headache, and did not join the party that was about to explore towards the planetary east. She lay down to rest. Within half an hour she was dead.

Everyone was recalled to the *Solarian*; and all exploration was suspended while Zeno attempted to discover the reason for her death. But his investigation was fruitless. Meanwhile, other members of the life-unit began to complain of headaches.

Faraday acted immediately. The entry-ports were sealed, and the starship was taken back to the five hundred mile orbit.

But it was already too late. Planet Three continued to take its toll.

Atlanta, Shannon, Montaigne, Carmel, Leonardo and Corunna died high above that green strip of land—so poor, yet so rich in potential—that they had hoped to colonize. Zeno stood by helplessly, watching the grim course of a sickness he could not understand; a disease in which he was unable to detect any physical agent.

A week later, during which there had been no more deaths, the survivors began to feel that they were safe, and began to consider the future.

After a series of seven useless and exhausting autopsies, after the depressing task of re-cycling the remains, Zeno stood one day by the observation panel and gazed down at the enigmatic surface of the planet that had destroyed so many of his companions. Presently, he was joined by Faraday, and then by Kepler.

"The first touch-down," said Zeno in a listless voice, "and it almost finished us . . . Is it worth while going on and on only to come up against something like this?"

Faraday followed his gaze to the green featureless plains. "Planet Three didn't kill them," he said. "I did—with being too bloody clever!" His face was gray; he seemed to have aged ten years.

Kepler gave him a furtive glance, a compassionate glance. "No," he said softly. "I have been thinking about that. You are wrong . . . Don't you remember refuting my argument with determinism?"

Faraday wore a thin smile. "You don't need to look for a back door for my conscience," he said roughly.

"Your conscience doesn't interest me," returned Kepler with spirit. "It just happens that determinism is the only solution. The memory had to be fulfilled."

Faraday suddenly held out his hand. "Thank you for knocking down my self-pity . . . But after this, I think the unit needs a new leader. You had better take over, Kepler. You are the best equipped."

"No."

"Why not?"

"Because I am not yet ready . . . And because I have faith in you."

Zeno turned from the observation panel. "Where the hell do we go from here?" he asked savagely.

Faraday glanced at Kepler. "Procyon?" he suggested.

"You are the leader."

Zeno began to laugh. "Take a good look," he said, jerking his thumb towards the observation panel. "As far as our generation is concerned, it is the first and last planet in the cosmos."

"For the generations to come," said Kepler, with a sudden conviction of foreknowledge, "there will be a darkness deeper than that between the stars."

Presently, the *Solarian* climbed out of orbit. The volatility rockets were cut out, and the star-drive took over, slowly building up velocity for the long elliptic fall.

The Companion of Sirius drifted leisurely astern, and the hard point of Procyon loomed on the starboard bow.

It was the beginning of a new era: the end of the fiftieth year.

Part Three

Then was not non-existent nor existent: there was no realm of air, no sky beyond it.
What covered in, and where? And what gave shelter?
Was water there, unfathomed depth of water?

THE RIG-VEDA: Creation

"I have had a most rare vision. I have had a dream, past the wit of man to say what dream it was: man is but an ass, if he go about to expound this dream. Methought I was —there is no man can tell what. Methought I was—and methought I had—but man is but a patched fool, if he will offer to say what methought I had. The eye of man hath not heard, the ear of man hath not seen, man's hand is not able to taste, his tongue to conceive, nor his heart to report, what my dream was. I will get Peter Quince to write a ballad of this dream: it shall be called Bottom's Dream, because it hath no bottom . . ."

SHAKESPEARE: A Midsummer-Night's Dream

GERMINAL

Proem

Lost in a frigid continuum of space and time, a sea of darkness and silence rippling to the impossible shores of eternity, the galaxies drift—nebulous, remote. They are vortices of starry plankton, bright illusions of life in the tides of a vacant ocean. For darkness is, was and shall be on the face of the deep.

But perhaps this compulsive futility is merely a single aspect of compulsive purpose. Perhaps, in some way, such illusions may achieve the threshold of reality.

Pursuing, then, this same vision of a cosmic ocean wherein the galaxies drift, a hundred thousand million suns are but a faint halo of astro-plankton. Distantly, they become a transient point of light, lost in the light-pricked currents of space, creating barely a surface ripple in time. They become no more than a brief, illuminated moment within the absolute perimeter of change.

Yet this minute radiance may itself be magnified into an infinite series of patterns. Then microcosms become macrocosms, revealing wonders that confound all perspective.

Between the beginning, if there could have been a beginning, and the end, if there could be an end, lies totality. Or perhaps there is simply a timeless change in which the first breath of creation and the last sigh of existence are indistinguishable. And out of this first breath, this final sigh, the cloudy nebulae are blown, condensing into hazy filaments of stars.

Presently, from the jostling and explosive mating of a billion swirling stars, planets issue. And again, cosmically, the moments of birth and death are not divided. For death is only a loss of radiance, and birth is only the beginning of a separate journey.

The fiery filigrees resolve into burning tears; and the tears harden in darkness and silence. All that remains is a few particles of ash gyrating blindly round the star from whose white womb they were drawn.

But once there was a star whose third planet, still warmed by the radiance of its parent sun, gave promise of a strange resurrection. For its ashen pallor deepened into a glowing green. So the dead microcosm became a living macrocosm to the beady eyes that explored its contours and the waking minds that tried to understand.

At last, with the emergence of the creature that was terrestrial man, another significant microcosm was created which, in turn, was macrocosmic to the individuals of its kind. Thus the infinite series of patterns was continued, revealing wonders that confound all perspective.

Perhaps, then, the compulsive cosmic purpose was hidden in sheer immensity. Perhaps the burning of a hundred thousand million suns conspired simply to one small miracle: the living of a hundred thousand million human lives. And perhaps so many deaths were necessary so that, ultimately, man and woman—together being couriers of immortality—might understand.

So that they might understand why the galaxies of starry plankton are created, sustained and consumed by fire; why the ashy diatoms of planets circle patiently round their dying suns; and why *homo sapiens*, bringing his own legend of the phoenix to the very edge of reality, should find birth and death and rebirth in the same celestial fire.

For man was star-born—conceived, perhaps, as the voice of stars; giving himself the task of answering the questions that were never asked. And man, the warrior, the wanderer, cannot achieve fulfilment until he accepts the twofold task of solving and accepting his own identity.

Man can never evade the intolerable burden and distinction of mind. And mind is so fashioned that it can never renounce the pursuit of meaning.

Perhaps it is part of the celestial paradox that only the microcosm of man and the macrocosm of mind can discover a purpose in the random drift of the galaxies. And perhaps it was the function of the stars simply to create mind.

For, without mind, there can be no meaning.

Chapter One

Perspective

The universe was empty, yet it was filled with the tantalizing brilliance of stars. The universe was silent, yet always there were the whisperings of ghosts. Time was without significance, yet moments trickled slowly as if from a slow leak in eternity. Space was immeasurable, yet each star was at the very rim of the cosmos. And the *Solarian* continued to drift, an infinitely small seed, through the dark valleys of creation.

But the seed was itself a universe, bound by the dimensions of hope, endurance and courage. It was a capsule of history, a pin-point miracle, a microscopic dream of resurrection . . . A message in a bottle, written by a dying race, and tossed into the black uncharted oceans of the night. A pathetic and magnificent gesture.

As the years of star-flight passed, it seemed as if the occupants of the *Solarian* had become no more than self-condemned prisoners of eternity, the last cadre of a race that could achieve neither total extinction nor the glory of rebirth. Generations came and went, stars waxed and waned; and still the *Solarian* challenged with small, fierce purpose the indestructible army of light-years.

Slowly, the list of star voyages grew, and was itself a testament to the endurance of the ever changing life-unit. For each voyage had contained decades of hope, of life and death, of patience and restraint beyond anything that had previously been demanded of human beings. And each voyage, for one reason or another, had ended in the same overwhelming despair. Each time, it was a despair that threatened to engulf the life-unit, to peel away the thin shells of sanity that encased all the separate tensions and frustrations of everyone in the *Solarian*. And each failure resulted in the inevitable toll of suicide, apathy or a spiritual retreat from realities that were too harsh to be faced without some violent reaction.

But always the life-unit pulled itself together—somehow. The suicides were re-cycled; the insane were given therapy or euthanasia, depending upon the possibilities of recovery; and eventually the apathetic, drawing upon their last intellectual or emotional resources, managed to return to at least an outward display of normality and so maintain their positions as functioning members of the unit. As always, the survivors looked towards the next star; and as always, they drew irrational confidence from the final article of faith that surely the next one must possess habitable planets.

It was rare for any individual to survive the disappointment of two useless voyages. For one thing, the crossing of the star-gaps, during the early voyages when the *Solarian* was only able to travel at low sub-light velocities, occupied usually the bulk of an individual's lifetime; and in some cases, the gaps were so wide that many members of the life-unit were born and grew old and died en route, never knowing the terrible privilege of discovering that the star they journeyed towards was barren, or that its planets were in some way unsuitable.

But the more formidable reason why few survived two voyages was that the disappointment of realizing that decades of endurance had come to nothing was a sensation which human beings might, perhaps, bear once in their lives, but rarely twice.

Although the entries recorded in the *Solarian's* star-log were dated according to the year of star travel in which they occurred, the members of the life-unit acquired the habit of using each star voyage as a unit of historical reference; a convenient demarcation of eras in the long limbo of stellar exploration. Thus, to the tenth generation life-unit, the Alpha Centauri voyage—long buried beneath an avalanche of light-years—was The Beginning; and its star-log had acquired the dignity and almost the allegorical quality of a book of genesis.

For the Alpha Centauri voyage, and the log that Newton had kept, came to be regarded even by the great-grandchildren of the original star voyagers as the beginning of the only real world in the cosmos.

Earth, whose history was still preserved on micro-film in

the archives of the *Solarian*, was no longer imagined as a real world, a planet with a rather unusual geophysical pattern that still rotated round one of the brighter stars in the black and limitless sky. It had become an almost religious concept; and the manner in which the *Solarian* had left Europe Three invoked a supernatural element; for Earth had assumed the status of paradise, and the way in which man had been forced to leave his natural planet seemed like an expulsion of fallen angels.

And, indeed, perhaps it was. For was not Earth—that legendary world of fertile continents, of iridescent oceans and mercurial skies—an actual paradise until *homo sapiens* squandered his creative heritage in orgies of destruction? And if man was forced to leave his terrestrial home because of the devastation he had brought about, was not that simply a judgment executed by the left hand of God? Or by Nature, or Destiny, or whatever force men may imagine that transcends rational experience?

As star after star yielded its barren answer to those who voyaged in hope of another planet similar to Earth, a new mythology grew.

Intelligent human beings take pride in possessing intelligent and reasonable attitudes; and the descendants of the *Solarian's* first life-unit were descendants of the intellectual élite of one of the last outposts of civilization on the dying Earth. But in adversity, intelligence alone cannot sustain hope. Ultimately, hope can be sustained only by finding purpose in adversity, by imposing a pattern on the fortuitous disasters of existence. Human beings, if forced to it, will compromise their intelligence to preserve their hope. And so it was with the occupants of the *Solarian*.

In the end, despite scientific rationale and logical explanation, the long succession of fruitless voyages inspired in the members of the life-unit an unconscious acceptance of the notion that they were, in effect, expiating the sins of mankind. They came to regard terrestrial man's indiscriminate use of the power sources he had discovered not simply as futile wastage and destruction, but as a deliberate and moral sin against Nature. And Nature had retaliated by driving the remnant of mankind into the outer darkness, there to be purified by suffering or to be annihilated by despair.

In the end, they came to regard the star voyages as primarily a series of endurance tests devised by Nature both as a racial punishment and as a means of inhibiting, by natural selection, the destructive element in man.

It was a religious attitude that was akin to philosophy; and its philosophical basis could be related to science. But above all, it afforded a way of deriving some positive virtue from the *Solarian's* ceaseless wanderings.

Nature—or whatever name is given to the universal *intent*—had been dissatisfied with the shortcomings of terrestrial man. For, though *homo sapiens* on his home planet had evolved a highly efficient technology, he had retained the proprietary and acquisitive attitudes of the peasant together with the lethal instincts of the carnivore. And the technology that might have heralded universal prosperity had been employed by peasant mentalities still dominated by the instincts of the killer.

Out in deep space, there were no more backward peoples to be exploited by machine-made civilizations, no problems of color or creed to be 'settled' by lynch-law or nuclear warhead, no political systems to regiment the mind or enslave the body. There was only a handful of survivors, lost in the immensities of space and time, slowly being stripped of the racial arrogance that had been built up over thousands of years: survivors who were literally being forced to abandon their inherited terrestrial prejudices for a kind of cosmic attitude.

For almost a thousand years, for over thirty stellar voyages lasting forty generations, the *Solarian* explored one tiny segment of the galaxy, searching for the planet that had come to be regarded as the Promised Land.

In spite of the sometimes disastrous failures, the miracle of hope continued to be renewed, but ever more slowly; until, by the twenty-fifth generation, the members of the life-unit began to discipline their personal hopes and despairs through a kind of spiritual non-attachment. It was not apathy: it was acceptance. An acceptance of all the apparent futility and suffering in the unshakeable conviction that behind everything there was purpose, and that the mystery of purpose would be revealed to the members of the life-unit only when the unit as a whole was ready to fulfil it. This attitude of mind had much in common with the spiritual detachment advocated long before by certain eastern religions on the lost planet of Earth. It was an attitude that preserved sanity at the expense of initiative, and that made the celestial entombment easier because the correct thing to do was to welcome its opportunity for discipline rather than abhor its limitations. And for a period of several decades, a mood prevailed throughout the life-unit wherein the discovery of a planet suitable for human life would have been regarded almost as an irrelevance.

This was referred to by later generations as The Time of the Great Introversion, when the life-unit turned inward upon itself and, collectively and individually, became more concerned with the significance of visions and spiritual experience than with objective realities. It was followed—perhaps inevitably—by a pendulum swing in which the emphasis lay upon extensive research with two main objectives: the lengthening of the individual life-span and the speeding up of star travel. The major problem of the first objective was not the retardation of physical aging, but the arrest of psychic regression—a factor which precipitated senility more than any other single cause. And the great problem of the second objective was the light barrier. Hitherto, the *Solarian* had voyaged at relatively low sub-light velocities. Hitherto, velocities exceeding that of light for physical objects had been regarded as a theoretical impossibility by generations of physicists; but a twenty-seventh generation leader of the life-unit, appropriately named Copernicus, developed a theory of sub-spatial stress which indicated that faster-than-light travel was, at least, not contrary to the fundamental laws of the cosmos. From that time forward, despite frustrating limitations of equipment and the facilities for experiment, the physicists and mathematicians worked to a single end.

The biologists and chemists might make their concerted effort towards the unattainable goal of immortality; but, ultimately, it would be left to the physicists to give point to whatever was achieved in that particular field. For the idea of a starship loaded with immortals destined to explore the rest of the galaxy at sub-light velocities was not one that the ever changing life-unit cared to contemplate.

The history of the *Solarian* might be traced simply as a pattern of stars—a tiny, enigmatic cipher inscribed transiently by a silver needle-point on the black page of space. But it was also a history of people, of the entire and evolving nucleus of what might yet expand—someday—into a society numbered in thousands or millions, or multiples of both.

The list of stars that figured in the *Solarian's* quest was small and easily remembered; for, at sub-light velocities, it would be hundreds of centuries before all the possible stars within a radius of a hundred light-years could be explored. But the list of human beings who took part in the star-journey was long, and the individuals—unless distinguished by some particular incident, discovery or decision—were not easily remembered. Their names, and the significant dates of birth and death, were all entered in the registers. But the entries for children who had died within even a few hours of birth occupied as much space and imparted as little information as the entries concerning people who had led long and useful lives.

Such sections of the registers as were more than a hundred years old were microfilmed and then destroyed, their pages being re-cycled to produce more paper or other useful materials. The star-logs shared a similar fate. But, fortunately, though they were primarily records of the progress of each star voyage kept by the leaders of the life-unit, significant events were often recorded in them. And the way in which each leader recorded his section of the star-log not only preserved indications of his personality and the emotional and intellectual climate of the *Solarian* during his leadership, but often left fragmentary accounts of the actions and attitudes of others of his generation.

But the most interesting records were those contained in personal diaries. Although none of these were preserved in the original and few were microfilmed, those that did eventually find their way into the starship's library provided a more or less continuous record of impressions and incidents—both trival and tragic—that reached back even to the original firing point. It was from these diaries that later generations were able to crystallize their persistently larger-than-life pictures of Newton and the people of the first star voyage.

A special significance attached to Newton and his generation, placing them in the category of demigods—or, more relevantly, fallen angels. For they were different from all successive members of the life-unit. Not only were they the first life-unit—a distinction not without its quasi-religious importance—but they were also people who had once walked upon the face of the Earth. People who had spent more than a third of their lives in terrestrial existence. People who had mingled with thousands of their own kind and who had acquired an incredibly rich store of planetary experience when the *Solarian* was no more than a project on the drawing boards in Europe Three.

It was, perhaps, inevitable that the passage of time should cover Newton and his contemporaries with a mantle of divinity, that they should be regarded by tenth and twentieth generation life-units with a mixture of awe and reverence, and that such incidents involving the first generation that were recorded in diaries should provide material for myth, legend and parable.

Newton himself came to be regarded as an archetypal leader. According to legend, it was by his decision alone that the threatened *Solarian* rose from Europe Three, confounding its attackers and implementing their death sentence as it ruptured the city's protective dome. According to legend, the rest of the life-unit, with the exception of Socrates, had allowed their judgment to be swayed by pity at the last moment; and only Newton's characteristic determination had enabled the starship to rise from the doomed planet and seek its cosmic destiny. Newton, then, was more than a leader: he was a lawgiver and protector. Presently, the adjective Newtonian was used to connote any superlative decision, action or suggestion. Its secondary use was related to the province of moral conduct. Supreme bravery or fortitude, unswerving integrity and resolution were regarded as examples of Newtonian behavior. And, in the face of tragedy or danger—as, for example, at the end of decades of star travel, when the target star was discovered either to be barren or to possess planets of doubtful value but still worth investigation—the life-unit was exhorted to maintain the 'Newtonian Norm'. Thus, the passing of centuries had translated Newton into an ideal of human conduct.

Socrates, on the other hand, developed as a symbol of ambivalence, of force that could be directed either for good or evil. Being the first of the *Solarian's* engineers, he was also regarded as the greatest. Again, according to legend, the original design of the starship's power unit was conceived by Socrates alone. The anonymous scientists and technicians of Europe Three were merely his laborers and apprentices. Socrates was the technical innovator, the organizing genius who had transformed the project on the drawing boards into an efficient and purposeful reality. To that extent, he was the archetypal discoverer and builder.

But Socrates was also the *Solarian's* first murderer. His

destruction of Rilke and his insane lust for power were represented as the demonic aspect of a mind that had been exerted beyond its normal capacity. In this respect, while his behavior during the early part of the Alpha Centauri voyage was unequivocally condemned, Socrates himself was to be pitied—the more so because of his later atonement and because of the device he perfected which enabled the starship to increase its velocity. His attempt at killing Jung on the navigation deck—an account of which Jung had left in his diary—was elevated to a struggle between titans: a symbolic conflict between physical evil and spiritual good.

For, over the centuries, Jung had assumed the stature of a mystic. His skills in psychiatry, surgery and medicine, outstanding though they were, became examples of a perfection unparalleled in the annals of star flight. Jung was the great healer, the incarnation of compassion.

In later generations, to use the word Socratic was to convey praise or warning or condemnation according to the context; but to employ the term Jungian was to employ an adjective the most accurate synonym for which would be the word sublime.

Of the first generation women, Troy was remembered as an ideal type of partner and as a person whose exceptional talent for handling the problems and development of children was rarely equalled. Alexandria also was immortalized—not as she had lived, but as a shadowy, tragic figure whose love for Newton had indirectly resulted in the death of Rilke.

Chapter Two

Precognition

By partnering with both Odessa and Granada, the other natural telepaths of his own generation, Kepler had introduced polygamy into a group whose numbers were small enough for it to constitute a serious danger. However, the relationship was founded less upon a sexual basis than upon a spiritual one. These were the first true telepaths to be born in the *Solarian;* and since there was no precedent for their treatment and education, they had been allowed to develop and exercise their powers virtually without restriction.

During later years, when other telepaths appeared, the major part of their childhood was devoted to mastering a form of inhibitory self-discipline which enabled them to extend or limit their powers by a series of mental 'control gestures'; and they were taught how to restrict their spiritual experience to within a well-defined sanity tolerance. The need for this had been adequately demonstrated by Kepler, who exploited his faculties beyond the limits of endurance.

Although, even before the Procyon voyage, tentative researches had been made concerning the possibility of faster-than-light travel, it was realized that the project could only be regarded as a long-term one, and that in all probability the *Solarian* would be doomed to many more light-years of 'conventional' exploration before the characteristics of sub-space were sufficiently investigated. But since he had assumed the leadership, Kepler had become convinced that, with the co-operation of Odessa and Granada, there was a chance of employing the special talents with which they were endowed to short-circuit decades of futile star journeys.

He had already received dramatic proof from his foreknowledge of the Sirius disaster that his telepathic experience could be extended in a limited way beyond the confines of space and time. It was evident that a kind of deep-level spiritual symbiosis existed between him and his two partners. It was evident also that the telepathic initiative belonged almost exclusively to Kepler, since neither Odessa nor Granada were ever able to receive anything other than a direct contemporary experience.

But as the three of them continued to explore their curious world of non-verbal communication, Kepler discovered that when Odessa and Granada remained spiritually passive, he could in some obscure way add their mental energy to his own and use it to deliberately project himself beyond the frontiers of normal telepathic experience.

A series of experiments during the early years of the Procyon voyage had enabled him to formulate a technique for travelling forwards or backwards through the memories of the various members of the life-unit. He had been wise enough not to divulge his ability to anyone except Odessa and Granada, from whom—even if their passive co-operation had not been needed—it was impossible to withhold any of his own experience or knowledge.

The significant fact was that the subject whose memories he explored—in either direction—was unaware that his privacy had been disturbed.

Although it was possible to approach the memories of a subject who was fully alert and even engaged in intense intellectual activity, Kepler found that the best results were obtained when the individual concerned was deeply asleep.

This process of what ultimately came to be called multistage cathexis had certain curious effects upon those who participated in it. Before Kepler could develop the cathexis, both Odessa and Granada had to relax voluntarily into a trance-like condition while Kepler, having assumed the 'womb posture' that seemed most conducive to good results, preserved a strange duality of conscious control and direction while totally oblivious of his immediate surroundings. Another result of the cathexis, which for obvious reasons was not discovered for some time, was that the subject thereafter experienced anticipatory recollection. That is to say, at fortunately infrequent intervals throughout the rest of his life he would remember certain incidents shortly *before* they happened.

When, at last, Kepler had sufficient confidence in his technique and as much knowledge of its manipulation as it was possible to have of such a peculiar experience, he decided to put it to practical use by deliberately 'pre-experiencing' the end of the Procyon journey through a suitable subject.

Meanwhile, extensive modifications of the *Solarian's* subatomic motor unit had permitted a further velocity increase of nearly forty per cent; and although the increase would have to be made slowly over a long period of time, so that the Procyon voyage would only be shortened by a year or two, it would be possible to cut any future voyage by upwards of ten years.

The partner of the engineer who had redesigned the power unit had just given birth to her first baby, a girl who was to be called Oslo. It was through this new-born child that Kepler proposed to pre-experience the end of the Procyon voyage. Then it occurred to him that it might be possible to achieve much more. Barring accidents, Oslo could be expected to live for about eighty years. If Kepler used the multi-stage cathexis to go forward to the end of her life, he would not only be able to acquire foreknowledge of Procyon but of the next star voyage as well—if there was one.

Ever since the time Kepler had given his warning about Sirius, he had been puzzled by efforts to reconcile determinism, free will, and pre-experience. But short-term experiments in cathexis had finally demonstrated that, contrary to his former belief, although it was possible to pre-experience the future, it was not fixed and unalterable. This had presented him with an apparent philosophical contradiction, until he realized that the future was an ever changing potential, constantly modified according to the law of causation and subject to sweeping changes by the introduction of new factors.

What he had experienced in the case of Sirius and subsequent 'controlled' experiments was not a definite future but a possible future: a future that could only be fulfilled if no new critical factors entered the network of casuality. Contrary to his assertion after the event, it would have been possible for Faraday either to bypass Sirius or not put any of the life-unit down on the Companion's Planet Three. It would have been possible, though, only if Faraday had believed Kepler. In so doing, he would have introduced a new factor into the causal chain, which would have affected the potential future and so averted the catastrophe.

Kepler had demonstrated this to his own satisfaction several times by pre-experiencing a near and trivial event of the future through a member of the life-unit and then revealing his knowledge to the subject—usually, all that was needed was a vague hint or suggestion. Almost invariably, the subject made use of the information—the new factor in causality—to 'change' his potential future.

Kepler's motivation, then, in using a multi-stage cathexis, was not simply to have foreknowledge of what was going to happen, but to have forewarning of what would probably happen if no new and significant causal factors were introduced into the situation.

If, therefore, using Oslo as a subject, he was able to have foreknowledge that Procyon was barren, it would be possible to use that very foreknowledge as a causal modification. In which event, the *Solarian's* course would be changed, and that aspect of the potential future would remain unrealized.

It was as if innumerable strands—causal lines—stretched out from everyone and everything into a literally unpredictable future. And in a single cathexis, Kepler was simply following out one of the strands.

Thus, in using the baby Oslo as a subject, Kepler would be able to follow a potential future through something like seventy or eighty years.

He did not tell the child's parents of his plan since, as previous experience had shown, the subject was only mildly affected by the cathexis. The psychological hazards involved in using the technique were Kepler's own problem. In previous short term projections, the effort required had frequently exhausted him for several days. In the present instance, he was proposing to systematically traverse the entire life-span of a human being.

Kepler planned to develop the multi-stage cathexis during the long rest period that was the equivalent of night aboard the *Solarian*. It was only then that the starship was really quiet; for in deep space it was unnecessary to keep a continuous watch.

Odessa and Granada were already lying in their contour-berths on the navigation deck, relaxing into the first stage of the trance-like state which was necessary before Kepler could channel their psychic energy towards cathexis. He had chosen the navigation deck for the experiment because it was normally one of the most deserted parts of the ship and because its atmosphere of spaciousness, aided by the observation panels through which a glittering array of stars was visible, seemed almost to inspire the cataleptic state into which Odessa and Granada would have to sink.

The subject, Oslo, was presumably asleep in the *Solarian's* nursery. But soon Kepler would enter her infant psyche and sink deep into a whirlpool of precognitive memory.

But before he lay down on his own contour-berth, Kepler looked at Odessa and spoke to her softly. There was no reply. He went to Granada's contour-berth and did the same. Both women were asleep with their eyes open. Gently, Kepler closed their eyes. Then he lay down himself and, with practiced discipline, began to empty his conscious mind of all irrelevant thoughts. Presently, all that remained was a growing and dominant image of Oslo. The visual image of the baby's face seemed to expand like a balloon, filling the *Solarian*, bridging the star gaps, obliterating the entire cosmos. And presently, there was an involuntary movement of Kepler's knees as he curled up into a tight human ball and assumed the characteristic foetal posture.

There was darkness and no feeling. Then the first sensation was of warmth—an incredible warmth, a red overwhelming warmth that was the feeling of comfort and semi-oblivion and fulness. There was an intimate, recognized smell; the touch of something warm and soft in the mouth, the spasmodic movement it inspired, the low warm noise that accompanied it.

The psychic force that was no longer Kepler but an abstract and purposeful fragment of his personality recognized the sweet scent of milk, the resilience of a nipple, the hardness of a full breast, the sound of Oslo's mother singing softly.

There was no time to waste. No time to waste in that infantile cosmos where every feeling was fierce and compulsive, where even joy and satiety were as sharp upon adult experience as pain. The nonpersonal probe winced dully as the sensations of babyhood poured over it lke a scalding waterfall. Then there was a brief orientation, and the probe willed inward towards its purpose.

Scenes flickered jerkily like a series of brief snapshots . . . An ego growing like a strange soft crystal. Meaning creeping visually through the shutters of the eyes, throbbing in the eardrums, crawling like a delicate insect along the spider web of touch and taste and smell.

Triumph! The understood word! The word repeated. More

words. Rippling nonsensical streams of words pouring through the ego as rays through a prism. The broadening spectrum of meaning. Occasional glimpses of the focus of reality. The universe through a burning glass, drawn to a pin-point moment of perception . . .

Walking, falling, walking, stumbling, walking, running, laughing . . . Love and hunger and love and anguish and love . . . And pain . . . Happiness, friendship, fear—all transformed and twisted now in the spinning cocoon of words.

The probe watched Oslo enter the world of childhood, watched as she grappled heroically with the problem that though the *Solarian* was the universe, yet was there a greater, darker universe outside.

Through her eyes, the probe watched the life-unit shrink from the stature of giants to that of normal men and women, as the child Oslo grew taller, older; as her perception grew quicker, her eyes brighter; as Procyon, the star ahead, grew brighter also, dominating the black sky.

Oslo was fond of the navigation deck. In adolescence she would spend much of her time there alone, daydreaming. Daydreaming of the green, the miraculously green and fertile planets that must surely belong to such a proud and fierce star. It was while she was weaving strange fantasies of planetary life as she gazed through the observation panels that Oslo received her first kiss. It was given and taken in darkness and silence by a boy called Alexander—the one whom she had expected; the one with whom she had already learned to speak the eloquent language of eyes. And the probe felt currents of fire in her body, felt them burn away the tattered fabric of childhood as Oslo knew the moments of joy and fear and sadness and love that conspire to create a woman.

The scenes no longer flickered. The whirlpool became a pit of time; and down it, the nameless personless probe fell like a stone towards the point of discovery when the woman Oslo would learn the secret of Procyon.

The day she partnered with Alexander, Procyon's system of planets was announced as a mathematical probability. A year and a half later, as the birth of her child became imminent, the *Solarian's* instruments had already detected six of the seven planets of Procyon A.

Oslo was filled with a double excitement; for it seemed as if the birth of her son—she was sure it would be a son—would coincide with the re-birth of humanity upon a new world. But the probe, the pure psychic force that was projecting through her life-span and of which she was no more aware than she was aware of the hidden face in her expanding womb, the probe knew that Oslo would not be present at the first planetary touch-down; for it had witnessed the unconscious preparation of her body, it had sensed the obscure psychic faltering that indicated the approach of death.

Oslo died of heart failure in childbirth some weeks before the anticipated planetfall; and in the moment of her dying, the probe—dominated always by its purpose and spurred by the apparent inevitability of failure—achieved what was no longer in the province of cathexis. It passed from the dying mother into the newborn child and endured once more the slow and agonizing process of individuation, waiting to learn the secrets of Procyon's seven planets.

Meanwhile, in the 'now-point' of twenty-three years before, the 'now' that belonged to another frame of time, another tapestry of reality, the infant Oslo slept restlessly in the nursery of a *Solarian* that was light-years ago; while Odessa and Granada lay trance-like in their contour-berths, and the vacant body that was Kepler retained its tight foetal pose.

But twenty-three years away in the potential future, Oslo was dead—already re-cycled—and her baby was not a boy but a girl to whom the name Cathay had been given.

Again, the probe endured all the irrelevancies of infancy and childhood until Cathay was old enough to understand the Procyon episode—by which time, Procyon was well astern, and the *Solarian* was gathering velocity for the long fall towards Vega.

Of the seven planets of Procyon, one was approximately the size of Earth and one the size of Jupiter, with roughly equivalent densities. The other five planets were all smaller than Mercury, and at such a distance from their sun as to make permanent occupation by anything other than a small self-contained life-unit impossible. Planet One, whose size approximated to Jupiter, was a steam-shrouded monster on one side and a dead ice-bound region on the other. It circled the parent sun once every two and a half terrestrial months, presenting always the same face to Procyon. Although there was a broad green band in the permanent twilight zone, indicating that Planet One already possessed at least primitive forms of life, it was impossible for the *Solarian* to touch down; for the planet, being three hundred earthnorms, would have crushed human beings to a thin layer of plasmic jelly by its tremendous gravitational pull. If advanced indigenous animal life did exist in the twilight zone, its skeletal system must have been able to bear fantastic stresses. So there was nothing for the *Solarian* to do but shoot out of orbit, after a short period of observation, and proceed to Planet Two.

Here, there was only one basic deterrent to the establishment of a community in the twilight zone (for Planet Two also presented one face only to its sun) and that was the total lack of atmosphere. But there was no reason at all why the *Solarian* should not make a touch-down and enable the life-unit to have the precious experience—which few of them could hope to have again—of walking upon the surface of a planet.

It was a bitter experience made even more bitter by the discovery of quite elaborate types of plant life which had adapted to living in a vacuum, and whose incredibly long and needle-sharp roots bored deep into the fissures of what seemed to be volcanic craters, there to extract and process the vital ingredients of life.

The surface of the twilight zone on Planet Two was something of an enigma, for it was pockmarked with craters of every conceivable size, whereas neither the hot face nor the cold face bore much disfigurement in that respect. The problem was so fascinating to the human beings who moved clumsily about the craters in their pressure suits that it was decided to make a low-level reconnaissance shoot round the twilight zone in the *Solarian*.

A complete photographic record was made, and this was examined after the starship had completed one revolution at a speed which was too fast for human beings to observe the terrain in much detail. The greatest surprise of all came when the cinefilm revealed unmistakable evidence of the ruins of two extensive cities on opposite sides of the twilight zone.

Here were the first signs of intelligent life that the *Solarian* had encountered in all the empty decades of star travel. The excitement of the life-unit rose to fever pitch. At first, there were wildly irrational hopes that despite the lack of air and the obvious antiquity of the ruined cities, there might yet be a few survivors somewhere on the planet—living, perhaps, in subterranean caves or under air-filled domes in much the same way as the inhabitants of Europe Three. But further photographic reconnaissance discouraged even the most optimistic members of the life-unit. Finally, it was decided to put the *Solarian* down near the larger of the cities for a short period of research.

The result was disappointing and, in a sense, tragic; for elaborate tests, involving atomic and geochemical techniques, established that the city must be at least sixty thousand earth-years old. The buildings, such as retained some semblance of their original shape, were mainly hexagonal; and some of them had obviously been several stories high.

But the greatest shock came when the mode of their destruction was definitely established. The craters that scarred the face of the twilight zone on Planet Two had their greatest numerical concentration around each of the cities; and when this was correlated with the fact that many of the stone buildings in the cities had been *melted* rather than knocked down, the life-unit was left with the inescapable conclusion that Planet Two, its cities, life and atmosphere, had been destroyed by a series of atomic wars. A series of wars, rather than one colossal battle, was postulated because of the great variance in the radioactive age of the craters.

By inference, the history of the civilization was slowly pieced together. The two cities must have been the victims of a conflict that had continued intermittently for about five thousand earth-years. But whatever bitterness had made them into enemies—whether it was religious, political, commercial or intellectual—neither side would compromise or accept defeat. And each had fought the other to a standstill, preferring mutual destruction to the triumph of one.

Now, all that remained of two civilizations that must once have been the equal of any on Earth were heaps of stone; distorting mirrors of fused rock; stains of oxydation and small piles of metallic dust that had once been great and wonderful machines; and a few curious ceramic fragments that still retained tantalizing hints of color and pattern and purpose.

Planet Two was a graveyard; and in spite of its fascination, the members of the life-unit realized that an attempt to colonize would be futile. For many of them, this would be the last time they could hope to walk upon the surface of a planet—even if only in pressure suits. And the knowledge that Planet Two was a world that had once been inhabited by intelligent beings, perhaps even humanoid in form, only made the situation more poignant. As the time allowed for the planetary exploration drew to its end, as the fragmentary and tragic evidence was pieced together to make only a vague and general pattern punctuated by too many question marks, the members of the life-unit were appalled by the futility of the long struggle for supremacy between the two city states; a struggle that had resulted in the use of such suicidal and terrible weapons as were capable of 'burning up' the entire planetary atmosphere.

Presently, the *Solarian* rose up from the surface and engaged in star-drive. But even when Planet Two was no more than a faint point of light and Procyon itself an ever-diminishing disk, there were many backward glances. Glances that were filled with the longing of those who were condemned to life-imprisonment in space; who, until the day they died, would see nothing in the universe but the slowly changing pattern of stars.

From a practical point of view, however, the time spent on Planet Two had not been wasted, for many useful minerals had been extracted to replenish the *Solarian's* slowly dwindling supplies. Although the star-ship was a closed biological system in which all waste material was efficiently re-cycled, small losses were inevitable; and the star-ship's power unit accounted for a slow but steady reduction of the total mass.

Thus, as the *Solarian* journeyed towards Vega, the probe that was no more than an extrapolated psychic force belonging to another dimension of existence learned from the widening mind of Cathay what had happened in the Procyon system.

Unsatisfied, restless, the probe reached deeper into the future, compulsively seeking the answer to questions that might never be answered. It watched Cathay's childhood flicker transiently on the screen of total experience; it glanced briefly at the crowded tumult of her adolescence; noticed vaguely that she had already partnered; and merely paused when she gave birth to her first child.

To the probe, all personal things were irrelevant. It reached only towards the next star. Towards Vega.

But, in the thirty-fifth year of Cathay's existence, the *Solarian* was close enough to Vega for a planetary check.

And the star was barren.

Without pause, the *Solarian* swept round in a wide power curve until, as the cosmos seemed to turn in a slow and stately dance, the next target star fell ahead of the ship. It was Altair.

Calculations had shown that, at maximum velocity, the

journey to Altair would take more than twenty-four years. With remote detachment, the probe noticed that the disappointment of Vega had aged Cathay subtly and devastatingly. It was aware that she would probably die before the starship explored the system of Altair. And because the probe was still dominated by the purpose of that far-off cathexis in another corridor of time, it tried to make the 'psychic jump' from Cathay to her son. But it could not. For it was locked to Cathay as surely as if it were an integral part of her personality.

Days flickered into months and years, and were swallowed in a single yawn of eternity. But to the probe, time was nothing and duration was all. It was necessary for Cathay to remain alive until the *Solarian* reached Altair; for then the probe would be able to return to its own time and place and psyche with the precognitive experience of three separate star journeys . . . It was necessary—but impossible.

For Cathay died suddenly while the starship was still three light-years from its target. And in the moment of her death, the probe snapped back across the gulf of decades that had yet to exist, like an elastic band stretched beyond breaking point. Instantly, it returned to the foetal ball that was Kepler; to the navigation deck that was still shrouded in the normal silence of the long rest period.

And presently, Kepler groaned. Then his limbs uncurled in a paroxysm of shudders. The icy sweat that drenched his body was unnoticed; the pain that racked him was irrelevant. For the regressive cathexis had demanded too much of those who had taken part in it. Kepler's orientation was broken. His conscious memory and rational powers had been unable to sustain such trauma.

The probe still possessed its fund of precognitive experience. In that respect, the cathexis had been entirely successful; but the probe had returned to a psyche that was unable to reintegrate it. And now it was caught in the swirling mists of amnesia, the random pockets of darkness that were slowly filling a mind too exhausted, too traumatized, to switch on once more the steady light of rationality. The probe was shouting—silently, urgently. But the only answer was a silence that lacked all urgency, in a mind that was too absorbed in the revelations of unmeaning.

Physically, Kepler was still alive; but as a functioning human being he was dead beyond hope of resurrection. Dead also were Odessa and Granada; for the extended cathexis had drained away all vitality, had broken down into psychokinetic energy even the nucleus of the ego. But their deaths had been a simple and painless transition from the comatose state into which they had already sunk; and were accomplished only at the moment of return, when the probe had drawn upon the last reserve of energy to return to its psycho-temporal origin. Odessa and Granada were peaceful in death, which had been a barely perceptible change in their last condition of living.

For Kepler, however, there remained a rhythm of dark and inward stresses that could only be resolved by euthanasia.

He continued to lie upon his contour-berth—not because he was unable to move, but because there was no assertive desire for movement—and the arrows of pain streaked through his body towards an oddly remote focus in the shrinking reality of his mind.

He had to wait several hours before any member of the life-unit ventured to the navigation deck. But time no longer possessed any relevance for him; and the external world was no more than a transparent myth.

The 'objective' duration of the cathexis had been a matter of minutes; but each minute had aged Kepler physically by a year. He was an old man now—an old man with a shock of white hair, with trembling uncoordinated limbs, with bright nonfocusing eyes, and with a voice that was no longer his to command.

He did not recognize a single face in the group around his contour-berth. For a moment, he gazed at each of them, as if he was expecting some sort of answer.

Then he made a tremendous effort to formulate his thought.

"Altair?" he whispered hoarsely. Then: "She died too soon . . . Too far from Altair . . . Altair?"

"Yes," soothed a woman's voice. "We will try Altair—if Procyon fails."

Suddenly, Kepler uttered a long cry of anguish—the anguish of a spirit that had momentarily recognized the futility of its own supreme effort. Then his limbs slackened, the arrows of pain became strangely gentle; and he died.

Presently, after a careful autopsy, after a long and useless inquest, the three bodies were re-cycled. A new leader of the life-unit was chosen. And the *Solarian* continued its smooth and uninterrupted fall towards Procyon.

Chapter Three

Transition

Thus, Kepler's attempt to cheat history, to short-circuit the tragically slow traversing of the star gaps, ended in defeat. But the life-unit continued; it continued to endure the penance of unimaginable journeys, to pursue the grail of racial survival, to flaunt its tiny challenge before the immensity of the universe.

Thus, over the centuries, the list of stars investigated by the *Solarian* became a roll of battle honors . . . Alpha Centauri, Sirius, Procyon, Vega, Altair, Fomalhaut, Arcturus, Pollux, Achernar, Regulus, Capella—each one taking its toll of life and hope. Each one adding decades to the total star journey. And each one—in spite of all the hazards it presented—unable to destroy the nucleus of civilization, the seed of greatness that had been flung out into the dark by a dying planet. The symbol of immortality that, infinitely small between the star gaps, yet contained a latent thunder which might one day shake the very galaxy.

For six terrestrial centuries after the death of Kepler, the *Solarian* pursued its galactic sweep at sub-light velocities. Stars waxed and waned, planets were discovered and discarded, leaders of the life-unit lived and died under the pressure of terrible decisions—decisions that had committed the voyagers to so many empty years. Hope came and went, but the quest continued; and even the discovery of barren or uninhabitable planets was better than none at all.

With the passing of the years, prolonged discipline and resignation had strange effects upon the life-unit. There was The Time of the Great Introversion—a period of several decades—when almost all the members of the life-unit rejected external phenomena for the satisfaction of inward experience and discovery. There was a danger that, as the cult of mysticism intensified, no one would bother to make decisions any longer or correct the *Solarian's* course; and, in fact, for a short period, there was little concern whether the starship reached a suitable system or fell to its fiery death in the heart of the nearest sun.

But the pendulum swung; and the Time of the Great Introversion was followed by The Awakening—a period of intense intellectual activity and far-reaching projects concerning the scope of future investigations.

Collectively, the life-unit had adequately demonstrated its ability to survive for an indefinite period. But while this was, basically, all that was necessary, it was felt that the individual life span was too short to permit emotional stability when each star journey occupied the major portion of a lifetime.

Researches into the nature of the aging process were carried out, with a view to extending the personal expectation of life so that the 'biological turnover' could be reduced, and so that human beings could never again be subject to the acute personal despair that in the past had overtaken those who had devoted their entire lifetimes to a single star voyage. Eventually, by dietary control and a system of spiritual exercises, the expectation of life was increased from decades to centuries. It was a mixed blessing and contained limitations as well as advantages. For one thing, the training for 'immortality' had to begin shortly after birth; and for another, although each new baby was subjected to the necessary physical and spiritual discipline that resulted in relative immortality, there was a high mortality during the years of infancy and childhood—until, in fact, the subject could appreciate and *accept* the purpose of the training. Finally, so long as an individual maintained the self-restrictions necessary to achieve immortality, he or she was condemned to remain sterile.

Presently, after much thought and much experiment, it was decided that the *Solarian* would not carry more than six Immortals at any given time, and that the rest of the life-unit would be restricted to a maximum of ten people with 'conventional' life spans and the gift of that other kind of immortality—the ability to procreate.

Meanwhile, significant advances had been made in the realm of physics. The twenty-seventh generation leader of the life-unit, Copernicus, had developed his theory of sub-spatial stress which, together with his general theory of motion, postulated that a moving body with a given and constant mass/velocity/deceleration ratio could actually *submerge* in space. The implications behind this notion were tremendous. If Copernicus was right, it would mean ultimately that the *Solarian* might be able to abandon its normal mode of space travel and enter the realm of space-time travel. And if Copernicus was right, a body submerging in space would, in relation to the *superficial* cosmos, cease to exist—until it emerged once more in normal space and thus became fixed in time.

Besides introducing a theory that could lead to the conquest of space and time, Copernicus also had the distinction of being the last mortal leader of the life-unit. He was succeeded by a mathematician and physicist called Thales; and then the benefit of immortality was apparent. Copernicus was able only to work on his dream of sub-space or space-time travel for barely three decades; at the end of which he was too old, too exhausted and too discouraged to continue.

But Thales, with the prospect of centuries before him, was not haunted by the terrible urgency that dominated those who could only expect the normal time span. For it seemed that, to the Immortals, even the subjective perception of time was different from that of the ordinary members of the life-unit. Having lost the ability to procreate and the secondary emotional stresses it entailed, the Immortals seemed to have attained a detachment, an objectivity of purpose and an acceptance of function that those who were relatively short-lived could not hope to appreciate. It was as if the Immortals had somehow shaken off or escaped all the fevers of the flesh; and in doing so, had found a satisfying form of expression in the creative journeys of the mind.

Thales, and a small ever changing team of mortal assistants, labored on the problems of sub-space travel for two and a half centuries. Meanwhile, new stellar explorations were begun and ended, resulting as usual either in the discovery of the barrenness of the target star or the inhospitability of its planets. But, unlike the short-lived, Thales rarely gazed through the observation panels, and even more rarely took the opportunity to step outside the *Solarian* when a planet suitable for temporary touch-down was reached. After each fruitless stellar search, it was his duty to select the new target star; but Thales performed this task almost perfunctorily, as if he knew it was a waste of time. As if he had some means of knowing that the *Solarian* could not possibly reach the true end of its journey by conventional space travel. As if, somehow, he realized that only through space-time travel could the real purpose of the starship be fulfilled.

So Thales concentrated on the physical and metaphysical problems presented by the possibility of using sub-space as a medium through which the *Solarian* might accomplish in the space of a megasecond what it had failed to achieve in the course of centuries.

And in the nine hundred and thirty-seventh year of star-flight, over thirty stellar voyages and forty normal span generations since the ship had left Europe Three, Thales perfected the curious instrument that, coupled to the starship's power unit, would enable the *Solarian* to submerge in space. It was not a large or impressive instrument. It looked like a fat copper cylinder that had been bolted carefully to the navigation deck. One end of it displayed a confusing array of dials, meters and switches, while a thick steel-sheathed cable extended from the other end like a monstrous tail. This contained all the leads that were to be connected to the ship's electronic nerve-centers, and to the control and timing devices on the main and auxiliary power units.

In one of his rare flashes of humor, Thales chose an elephantine name for the instrument it had taken so long to conceive, prove theoretically, and build. He called it a selective cosmometer.

During the final months of construction, everyone in the *Solarian*, whether directly connected with the cosmometer project or not, had done his best to appreciate the theory of operation. The intellectual ability of Thales was unquestioned; for even among the Immortals, his mastery not only of his own special studies but of such new sciences as electro-psychology and gene-mechanics was rarely equalled. And so the life-unit came to share his confidence that here, at last, was the instrument to end the *Solarian's* journey; the machine that would obliterate the nightmare of endless light-years, and so allow the life-unit to fulfil its original purpose.

As the date set for the 'cosmic dive' drew nearer, a new air of optimism permeated the ship; and the *Solarian's* library and micro-records were put to constant use by people engaged in research on planetary lore, the mysteries of climate, and the techniques of pioneering. On the final day, the excitement reached an unprecedented pitch, disturbing even the customary detachment of the Immortals. And the four small children in the unit had already touched down on an imaginary earthnorm planet, there to construct a base camp prior to the miraculous treat of 'looking for animals'.

Thales had asked everyone to assemble on the navigation deck a short time before deceleration, since the contour-berths on the navigation deck were the most efficient in the ship, and also it would be easier to control any last-minute tendencies to panic. When they were all together, he decided to pass the time until deceleration point by giving a short résumé of the function of the selective cosmometer.

For perhaps the third or fourth time in his life, Thales was aware of personal tension. But as he looked round the semi-circle of expectant and preposterously confident faces, his own tensions were dissipated; and his last-minute, irrational doubts were extinguished by the obvious faith of those who had worked with him on the project.

"As you all know," he began, smiling at a couple of nine-year-olds who had been solemnly discussing plateaux of reality, "matter is a form of locked-up energy. That is an item of knowledge which was commonplace even with our distant ancestors on Earth. What you may not know is that Newton, the first leader of this life-unit, suggested shortly before his death that energy might be a form of locked-up space. This was the great clue that set later generations of physicists upon the track of the coefficient of space-time in relation to the given stress of matter.

"Some generations ago, Copernicus advanced the notion that, as matter and energy were interchangeable, so also energy and space were. The mathematics that supported his argument are too complex to understand unless one is a natural adept; but a very simple demonstration of his thesis is found in the relationship between the diminution of cosmic mass, due to radiation, and the so-called expansion of space.

"The cosmometer we have designed has a twofold purpose. It is an instrument that may be regarded as a kind of key that will open the door separating our present scheme of reality from the multiple realities of past and potential conditions of the cosmos. Briefly, it will enable the *Solarian* to convert from an actual molecular pattern into a potential molecular pattern, within the frame of sub-space.

"The second function of the cosmometer is to define and

seek our *direction* while we are in sub-space. This is done by means of a spatial homing device which has been programed to recognize the conditions in which it would be favorable for the *Solarian* to emerge in space once more. As a matter of fact, the cosmometer is programed to define our direction/deceleration crisis only when we would emerge within half a light-year of a Sol-type sun possessing one or more Earthnorm planets.

"I must emphasize that while we are in sub-space, time as we know it has no significance whatsoever, and the length of our submersion cannot be measured by any instrument that depends upon spatial movement. The *interval* will have a different subjective value for each of us; and only when we are in normal space-time once more shall we be able to calculate the temporal displacement. The final point that I would like to make is that we may surface either in the past or the future, many thousands of light-years away from deceleration point. Conceivably, we might find ourselves in a different galaxy. In fact, all that may be relied upon is that we shall surface near a Sol-type sun possessing Earthnorm planets."

When Thales had finished, there was a brief silence. Several pairs of eyes glanced apprehensively at the ship's electrochron, which indicated that there were four and a half minutes left before the decelerative transition.

"Is there any possibility of error in the cosmometer?" someone asked hesitantly. "I mean, might the *Solarian* surface too near a sun, or something like that?"

Thales regarded the questioner gravely. "There is always the possibility of error," he said. Then he smiled. "There is even the possibility that the whole theory of sub-spatial transition is no more than a mathematical abstraction and a practical illusion. But these are possibilities not probabilities. And the overwhelming probability is that the selective cosmometer will fulfil the function for which it was designed."

"But what happens if the *Solarian* fails to surface after transition?" persisted one of the younger members of the life-unit.

Thales laughed. "The point is, in that case, that nothing at all would happen. We should continue to remain nonexistent in terms of mass and space and time." His eyes twinkled, "That seems to pose an interesting metaphysical problem. Would it then be possible for us to be aware of our non-existence?"

There was a general volley of laughter. But it was abruptly terminated by the voice of the auto-announcer.

"Sixty seconds to transition!"

"Check the safety belts," ordered Thales.

Each member of the life-unit was now lying in his contour-berth, secured by cross-webbing.

"Forty-five seconds to transition!"

A child whimpered, and clutched the doll that had suddenly become a talisman.

"Thirty seconds to transition!"

It was too late for fear or regret; too late to think of resetting or neutralizing the cosmometer, of taking more time to understand the nature of this, the ultimate journey; and too late even to remember those other journeys made by the *Solarian*—the long, silent falls to nowhere, the dark years of limbo between star and barren star.

"Fifteen seconds to transition!" said the auto-announcer in the same metallic tone it had used for so many countdowns in conventional decelerations. *"Ten, nine, eight, seven, six, five, four, three, two, one—zero!"*

And then there was a faint and curious echo, as of laughter in a vacant room. Then silence.

A ripple seemed to pass through the entire ship. A ripple of unreality that would break only when it reached the shores of some infinitely wide sea.

To the members of the life-unit, it was as if the *Solarian* and they themselves were dissolving like insubstantial shadows before a hard and penetrating light.

And the light was the light of Transition—the cosmic dawn light, a grey aureole of emptiness set as a halo round the misty perimeter of unbeing.

Time was nothing. Space was merely a legend—a receding myth that once might have contained all the ghostly shapes of galaxies that ever filled a shrunken ball of darkness.

Time was nothing. The past and the future were simply abstractions without meaning—cabalistic ciphers written invisibly across the great wall of non-existence.

Time and space were suddenly unborn, and Transition was all.

Then, without any warning, in a blinding overwhelming torrent of light-years, Transition broke. And the *Solarian* surfaced once more in space.

From the shores of an infinite sea, the ripple rebounded

until it had shrunk into the sharp point of reality. The echo changed back into laughter . . .

And it was the sad, thin laughter of human beings who had achieved the absolute resurrection; who lay in their contour-berths and gazed with the eyes of frightened children through the navigation deck's observation panels. They saw the strangely reassuring certainty of stars; and the miracle of a hard disk of fire, dominating the black sky, justifying the almost forgotten agony of faith.

No one spoke. For, at such a moment, there was nothing to say. But eager eyes had already noticed the peculiar color and intensity of the nearer stars. And an element deeper than intuition recognized the green and crimson miracle of planets.

Chapter Four

Renascence

The *Solarian* fell towards Planet Three, the green planet, like a slowly falling seed—a seed that was fulfilling its destiny; begotten of earth, and to earth returning. And what had been a way of life for forty generations of star-born human beings would, in retrospect, seem to be no more than a chrysalid state—the quiescent interval between larva and imago; the spiritual metamorphosis of *homo sapiens* . . .

For, in destroying the planet that was his natural home, terrestrial man had violated his own destiny. But before he was himself destroyed, the instinct for racial preservation had inspired him—in a brief blaze of genius—to offer his seed to the dark hazards of space and time, to the remote indifference of the stars. Terrestrial man had met his end; and in doing so, he had created the possibility of cosmic man and the hope of a new beginning.

Planet Three belonged to a large system; but it was the only living planet and the only one capable of accepting human life. It was about eight light-minutes from the parent sun, whose harsh radiation was softened by the planet's cloudy blanket of atmosphere.

The *Solarian* remained in orbit at an altitude barely above the atmosphere while a preliminary study was made of the surface conditions. Four-fifths of the planet were covered by iridescent oceans that seemed—even at such a distance—to proclaim mysteriously the life that was hidden in their depths. Most of the continental masses and nearly all the islands, large and small, were richly green with vegetation. Only the polar regions sported white, blinding expanses of frozen water.

Planet Three was indeed Earthnorm—except that there were no dead cities, nor was it dominated by the endless stretches of desert that had swallowed all living things in the world of Europe Three. And, like the Earth that was no more than a hazy and almost incredible legend, it possessed a satellite—an airless satellite that was barely one and a quarter light-seconds away . . .

Newton—or any of his generation—would have known. A glance at the continental masses would have told him; and before that, the pattern of planets; and even before that, the juxtaposition of the constellations. But Thales had to check the ancient star charts, the micro-records of the first years of star flight.

The cosmometer itself could give no indication. Its functions were limited to precipitating Transition, to taking the *Solarian* into sub-space; and there, in the limbo where all possible universes maintained a condition of potential co-existence, to selecting the pattern of a Sol-type sun with one or more Earthnorm planets.

It was only when Thales checked the old star charts that he understood.

The selective cosmometer had operated with perfect efficiency. In sub-space, its selectivity programing was confronted with the sub-spatial stress data of all possible stars in all potential conditions of existence. It had obeyed its coding literally. It had selected the star and the planet that corresponded most closely with the electro-coded description with which it had been programed.

Therefore, it had selected the Sun and the Earth.

But because the cosmometer had been programed to select at maximum life-bearing potential, it had caused the *Solarian* to emerge from sub-space in the proximity of Earth not as it was in the last days of Europe Three, but as it was fifty thousand years *before*.

Thales called a meeting on the navigation deck. He had chosen the navigation deck intentionally since, through its observation panels, a great segment of the planet could be seen. At the time he had chosen, the *Solarian* was on the dark side; and the misty stretches of the ocean 'below' glowed strangely in the moonlight. But presently, as the starship pursued its orbital course, it would create its own sunrise; and the continents would appear to roll by in a blaze of light.

Thales looked carefully at the assembled life-unit, reading the expressions on their faces as they gazed through the observation panels at the one suitable planet that had been discovered by the *Solarian* after a thousand years of star travel and the timeless moment of Transition. It was, he thought, an ironic situation—with the irony upon a cosmic scale.

"We are looking at a planet," he began unemotionally. "We are looking at the kind of planet that has been sought by the *Solarian* for more light-years than any of us cares to contemplate. We should do well to look carefully at this planet because there is a terrible decision to be made."

"What kind of a decision?" The question was asked by a girl called Eden, who had recently taken charge of child education.

"The decision to stay or to continue our search," answered Thales calmly.

There was a sudden murmur of surprise; but with equal suddenness, it stopped, as if a switch had been thrown.

"Why must there be such a decision?"

"Because the planet we have found is Earth . . . It is difficult to accept, isn't it? And difficult to believe that we should not immediately have recognized the world on which our ancestors lived. But the *Solarian* has been in deep space long enough for Earth to have shed its reality, long enough for it to become a myth. And when a myth is suddenly and unexpectedly substantiated, it is understandable that human beings should be unable to recognize it. For us to have recognized Earth would have been a harder feat than for Newton to have recognized Europe Three from records and statistics that were compiled hundreds of years before his birth . . . You see, we have been subjected to a temporal regression."

How long? No one had asked the question, yet it seemed to thunder through the *Solarian*, seemed to reverberate and echo in mind after stunned mind.

"We have found Earth," continued Thales quietly, "approximately fifty thousand years before the last civilization destroyed itself. We have reached an Earth that has yet to endure the conquest of *homo sapiens*. We have reached a dawn planet where the forests and jungles are teeming with life, and rich with unimaginable potential. Our tragedy—or perhaps it is our strength—lies in our foreknowledge. For we are already aware of future history. That is why we have to make our decision."

Again there was silence. A silence that was loud with tne avalanche of unspoken thoughts of people who were recalling all they had endured, and contemplating the fantastic reward of their endurance. And during that awful silence, the *Solarian* passed from the dark side of the planet and over the seaboard of a continent that was bathed in sunlight.

"It would be possible to re-program the cosmometer," suggested Thales. "It would be possible to inhibit its selectivity in such a way that the *Solarian* could never approach Earth, at any stage of its existence, again. If you are prepared to undergo Transition once more, we should be able to find a suitable planet in some other part of the galaxy—perhaps even in some other galaxy . . . This is not a decision that I can make alone. It is a decision in which we must all share."

"Surely there is another factor that we ought to consider." The young man who spoke was a biologist called Descartes. "Earth's future, as it is recorded in the *Solarian's* archives, belongs to the universe we experienced before Transition. We know that in the absolute condition of timelessness, from which the cosmometer selected the pattern of events for which it had been programed, all *possible* conditions of the universe are co-existent. Therefore, Earth is capable of the future not only as it occurred in the time-sector that produced the *Solarian*, but of an infinity of futures. If we touch down now, with the knowledge and skills at our disposal, we may perhaps modify the future."

Thales smiled. "That is true. But we may not be able to modify it so much as you imagine."

The girl Eden had been listening attentively; but all the time, her eyes were fixed upon the tempting patterns of life that, from a few hundred miles, looked like subtly changing hues on the skin of a ripe, celestial fruit.

"I am not very sure of the metaphysical aspect," she said slowly, "but it seems to me that, if we did touch down on Earth, we might so change the course of events that the kind of civilization that ended with Europe Three would never exist. In which case, fifty thousand years from now the *Solarian* would not be built, and therefore we ourselves could not have any reality . . . I know it sounds absurd, but how can it be otherwise?"

Thales laughed. "You are forgetting the peculiar nature of Transition. By experiencing Transition, that is by passing through sub-space, we became completely detached from our normal space-time orientation. In fact, we left what was then our *actual* universe to seek a potential cosmos. You see, the absolute nature of Transition contains an infinity of universes, an infinity of time, and an infinity of possible futures.

We have not simply travelled back in time. We have passed from one cosmic sequence into another. As far as the old cosmos is concerned, our reality if extinguished. We have entered, by Transition, a new sequence . . . There are so many possible worlds; and if, in this one, we so affect the history of Earth that Europe Three is never built, that does not affect our own existence. For the causal network that linked us to Europe Three was completely broken by Transition."

Eden still seemed skeptical.

"It is true," said Descartes. "*If* we establish ourselves on Earth, even though we substantially affect the future that is—or perhaps I should say *was*—part of our history, nothing we do can affect our present reality; for as Thales says, we are now in a different sequence. There is a mathematical proof of this. I don't understand it very clearly myself, I'm afraid. But I have seen it demonstrated with simple analogies."

Then Thales claimed the attention of the life-unit once more. "There is no logical reason why we should not touch down on Earth, but there may be a psychological one. Perhaps we know too much, and perhaps our knowledge will so inhibit our behavior as to bring about a spiritual or intellectual paralysis. We must remember also that primitive man is already upon this planet. Sooner or later, if we establish a community upon the Earth, we shall come into contact with those remote ancestors of ours. Then if, for example, we are attacked, how shall we reply to crude spears and arrows and axes? Shall we obliterate the attackers with atomic weapons? That would surely be the final tragedy: that we, the descendants of those who fled from a devastated planet, should return to begin the wastage in a different time sequence."

Thales paused, and gazed at the semicircle of faces intently. "But there is an even greater problem," he continued. "Let us suppose that we are able to establish a friendly relationship with these people. What shall we do then? Shall we teach them skills that might have taken thirty or forty thousand years of evolution to develop normally? Shall we teach them methods of storing food so that they shall not go hungry? Shall we show them how to triumph over their natural enemies, how to make comfortable homes, how to organize communities? Shall we teach them how to plant grain, how to care adequately for their newborn, how to keep records, to make clothes and tools and utensils, how to avoid pestilence?

"And what, then, of ourselves? Shall we adapt our own standards of living to planetary existence? Shall we indulge in unrestricted procreation so that presently we shall have the nucleus of a new civilization? Shall we, living on the same planet as these primitive creatures, use our sciences and our machines to produce, maintain and improve a way of life which, perhaps, they could never hope to equal?

"And should we, then, remain aloof—fencing ourselves in with deliberately inspired tabu, magic and superstitious dread? We could so easily make them learn to fear and avoid us. We could preserve ourselves as an intellectual, spiritual and physical élite. But then, sooner or later, they would break down the tabu. They would develop their own civilization, their own machines. And, sooner or later, there would be a trial of strength—a return, in the end, to atomic weapons . . .

"*If* we decide to touch down on Earth, instead of enduring Transition once more, these are but a few of the problems that we shall have to face. First, however, we must make our decision—aware of what it entails. As I have said before, this is not the kind of decision that may be made by any leader of the life-unit. The responsibility for it must be accepted by us all. Perhaps you would like time to think about it . . ."

Even as he finished speaking, it was possible to see through the observation panels the twilight zone appearing over the rim of the world. Presently, the *Solarian* would be passing above the night side once more.

"We are suffering from an overdose of time already," said Eden with emotion. "A history scaled in light-years and culminating in Transition. If we have to make a decision, let us make it now. More time will only increase our tension. And if, in the end, we decide to endure another Transition, the departure will only be more painful because we shall have had time to store in our hearts a clear memory of the planet that was—or is—the home of man."

There was a subdued murmur of agreement. Thales looked carefully and slowly at each of the faces that he knew so well.

"I had hoped that we should want to decide now. Although we might gain clarity of thought by taking more time, any delay would—as Eden has said—make it more difficult . . . Therefore, I ask those of you who believe that we should set the *Solarian* down on Earth, accepting all the problems that await us and full responsibility for the outcome, to raise your right hands."

For a moment or two, no one moved. Then, one by one, each member of the life-unit raised his or her hand—even to the children.

Thales said quietly: "This, then, is our abiding decision: that as, in a remote sequence, we were created of the Earth, so, in this sequence, we shall return to the Earth, endeavoring to act for the universal good, so that all human kind may profit by our emergence: and so that the terrestrial men and women who conceived, built and launched the *Solarian* did not do so in vain. And this is the decision of us all."

"This is the decision of us all." The final words were repeated softly by almost everyone present; and suddenly, strangely, the atmosphere on the navigation deck took on a religious solemnity, as if the steel and hiduminium shell had been transformed into a small temple. For a while, no one spoke; and all eyes were turned to the darkly glowing face of Earth—seeking the answer to a question that could only be answered, if at all, after thousands of years.

At length, Thales spoke once more: "So be it . . . There is no reason, now, why we should remain in orbit any longer. As soon as we have selected a base area, we will touch down. But first, we must all be clearly aware what our decision entails.

"We cannot—we dare not—put down on Earth, regarding ourselves as a race apart, a small group of highly civilized beings able to dominate easily the scattered tribes of men or sub-men with whom, in the end, we shall have to live in contact. It would be possible for us to select an area of the Earth which may not be explored or colonized for a very long time. But to do that would be a mistake; for in cutting ourselves off, we should be evolving our own separate world. And each year that passes would make approach or reconciliation all the harder. Our own sciences and culture would be expanding too fast and in directions that are not consonant with the responsibility we have accepted.

"I propose, therefore, that we touch down on the continent that was once called Eurasia. I propose that we select an area in which, as the microrecords show, there will be considerable movement of the nomadic tribes and families. I propose also that, when we are accustomed to planetary life, we abandon the *Solarian* both as a fact and as a symbol There will be a great temptation to continue using the starship as a base, a refuge, a laboratory and a home. But, in doing so, we should add to rather than diminish the barriers between us and *them*.

"I do not think it would be wise or necessary for us to seek to establish immediate contact with them; for they will discover us quite soon enough. But, when the time comes, we must be ready. We must be ready to greet them and regard them not as inferior creatures, but as beings who share the same blood heritage as ourselves, and with whom we must share a common future—if there is to be any future at all.

"We have travelled through many light-years and the long moment of Transition to meet them. They have endured a million years of forests and fevers, of hunger and compulsive striving so that they may raise their heads to the sky and walk on two feet. Which, then, is the greater journey?

"Finally, I must put before you some bitter facts concerning touch-down. Shortly afterwards, probably in the first months, we so-called immortals will die. Our way of life is not suited to endure the stresses of planetary existence for long. You who are left will have to contend with all the natural hazards of life. You will have to learn to react swiftly and positively to danger, to live on food that is not the product of controlled biosynthesis or hydroponics, and—hardest of all—to use natural resources rather than create your own.

"Some of you will die of diseases that will take their toll until natural resistance is developed. Some of you will pay a terrible price for your inability to interpret forest lore. But those of you who survive, learning to accept all the problems of terrestrial existence, to face the pitiless challenge of Natural Selection without being afraid or degraded, you will be the few who are privileged to take all that we have to offer to those who are waiting and who have yet to understand.

"And you will offer them no short-cuts to civilization, or machines that they are not yet ready to use. You will offer them, by example, the only gift we have that is worth the taking. The only power that may ever avert the ultimate devastation of this planet. You will offer nothing more than compassion—knowing that it may be rejected for thousands of years, knowing that it may always be rejected, or seen only as weakness. For mankind may survive and live without machines, and still be civilized. But without compassion, the human race can only elaborate upon the futile cunning and the barren intelligence of the great apes."

When he had finished speaking, Thales turned from the life-unit and gazed once more through the observation panels at the dark moonlit radiance of the largest ocean on Earth. The scene was incredibly beautiful; and, until the continents swung round, there was the strange illusion that Earth was no more than a warm celestial tear-drop—falling, always falling through a darkness without end.

One by one, the members of the life-unit left the navigation deck; some to relax, some to carry on with routine duties, and some to prepare the starship for an imminent touch-down. But Thales remained there, motionless, gazing at the Earth, thinking of an experiment whose end was unpredictable; an experiment of which he would only live to see the beginning.

But there was also the consolation of having seen an end—an end to all the pointless journeys, to the great inter-stellar silences, to the limitless oceans of darkness, and the deep inward currents of doubt.

To have seen the end was something: to witness the beginning would be enough.

Thales stayed there until, once more, the edge of the world took fire, heralding the *Solarian's* approach to part of a massive continent that lay under the oblique magic of the dawn light.

So it always was, he thought, and so it always would be. The end and the beginning joined together; and, without each other, meaningless. Thus, ultimately, there never could be an absolute end; just as there never could have been an absolute beginning. There could only be a continuous unfolding.

Destinations and origins, arrivals and departures, were arbitrary points, conceived merely to satisfy a desire for order and orientation in the mind of man. But, as always, there was the deeper desire for a sense of purpose. And purpose could be found not in arrival or departure, in the beginning or the end, but only in the manner of the journey; the spirit of the voyagers; the latent and manifest patterns of beauty locked in a single seed . . .

Epilogue

The forest was never silent, for the forest was rich with life. And the life-forms, multitudinous, diverse, were each compelled by a single purpose and a single inalienable right. For each strove to create and increase its own kind, regardless of the obstacles in its path and merciless to the enemies it might overcome; and each strove first to consolidate, then to expand its tiny kingdom in the ceaseless anarchy of the forest.

Thus, since the dawn of life, every creature—from the enduring and lowly pattern of the amoeba to the transient despotism of tyrannosaurus rex—had subscribed to the fundamental law of life. Each had claimed the right to survive and develop—if it could—and each had faced the penalty of extinction if it could not.

Only the enigmatic creature called Man would ever be prepared to challenge this basic law; for Man had that in him—be it the seed of madness or the seed of greatness—which compelled him to challenge everything, including the very conditions of existence. What other creature but Man would kill not for food or sport but for ideas? What other creature but Man would cherish the sick, the injured and the aged of his own kind? What other creature possessed such scope for cruelty or compassion? What other creature would ever need the gift of tears and laughter?

Lost in the heart of the forest was a high, tapering column of hiduminium and steel, its sharp nose still clear of the rising sea of foliage by which it was surrounded. But already from the earth tough and relentless climbing plants were weaving a green network which, in the course of time, would enshroud the *Solarian* completely, hiding it for ever from curious and startled eyes.

And presently, as the trees fell and the forest changed, as the vagaries of climate slowly altered the contours of the

Earth, so the *Solarian* would fall and be changed into an eroding sepulchre of ghosts and miracles, under the weight of decaying vegetation and the greater weight of centuries.

The Chinless Ones had seen the starship many times. And each time they had fled, returning never by intention but only by accident as they followed a wounded animal or sought the large sweet berries of the cool season. And each time, the Chinless Ones were inspired by the same overwhelming terror; the same unreasoning dread that made them forget everything—berries, animals, roots—in the urgency of flight.

Later, the Upright Ones, on their long migrations from the southeast, also encountered the starship. But they did not take to their heels so quickly. They stayed and gazed and poked; and scratched their shaggy heads and wondered—until they were diverted by other and more immediately useful things such as berries, animals, roots . . .

Some distance to the north, the descendants of the *Solarian's* life-unit had established their community by the side of a river. In the first years after touch-down, death had taken a grim and steady toll until, at times, it seemed as if the survival of the group was an impossibility. But slowly—with tragic slowness—the birth rate rose to equal, then exceed the death rate. Until, finally, a community of Earth-born men and women, to whom star-flight was barely more than a tribal fantasy, learned to accept the ruthless conditions of the forest where sharpness of eyesight and speed of movement were assets infinitely superior to a knowledge of theoretical physics or plant ecology.

But though the group now wore the skins of animals and lived in simple huts, though they hunted with spear and arrow, and crossed the river in hollowed logs, the rich store of knowledge that had been carried in the *Solarian* was not lost. The disciplines it had stimulated, the processes of thought it had inspired were still alive—dormant, waiting. Waiting, as the group waited, for the time when men would be ready to assimilate such knowledge and from it distil wisdom.

Already, there had been contact with the Chinless Ones. Many times, in recent years, their slouching ape-like forms had been seen on the far side of the river. Although the life-group had made friendship signs and had offered food, the Chinless Ones had kept their distance. But sometimes they stole food during the night. And once they stole a child.

That was a time of testing for the People of the River. Their first impulse was to track down the Chinless Ones and annihilate them, or so punish them that they would never again venture to that part of the forest. But then they remembered what it was that their ancestors had brought to offer on their return to Earth. And there was no chase, no vengeance. Only sadness, as they realized that there would be heavier burdens . . .

And there was pity, also, for the Chinless Ones who, whatever the People of the River might do, were doomed to annihilation at the hands of the Upright Ones—the True Men who were already moving from the southeast.

At last, there came the day for which the People of the River had waited—the day of their first meeting with the Upright Ones.

Five of the People were out hunting. And, in a glade near the river, they had made their kill—a type of red deer whose flesh was uncommonly good when it had been exposed to the embers of a wood five. The deer had been slung on to a branch so that it could be carried back to the river. But as the People were moving away with their prize, a faint hiss was heard. One man fell to the ground, a crude spear protruding from his chest. Another spear rattled harmlessly against a tree.

The People stopped suddenly, and raised their bows. There was nothing to be heard but the moans of their dying companion. Someone tried to take out the spear, but it had lodged in the rib cage; and the wounded man was already beyond help. Presently, his moans faded into a quiet spasm of coughing. Then there was silence.

The People crouched by the body of their companion and the body of the deer. Four iron-tipped arrows pressed tautly against bow strings. Four pairs of eyes systematically scanned the undergrowth.

Then, at the far end of the glade, three of the Upright Ones appeared. They carried only axes and spears. The People could have annihilated them. But even as the bows were drawn, the leader of the hunting group made a sign to his crouching companions. They remembered the Gift, and understood what it would mean.

And, after a moment's hesitation, the leader rose, standing upright. Simultaneously, three spears at the end of the glade were raised for hurling. Again slowly, the man of the People began to walk towards the spears. They were three sharp fingers of destruction pointing steadily at his chest.

After a few paces, he stopped. He tried to smile at the Upright Ones, hoping that they might understand the language of a smile. Then, deliberately, he placed his bow and few remaining arrows on the ground at his feet. He smiled once more at the Upright Ones, then pointed to his own discarded weapons.

Suddenly, surprisingly, one of the Upright Ones laid down his own spear. He, too, smiled. But the others did not move. Their spears still pointed unerringly.

The man of the People hesitated, thinking of all the wounds that would have to be given and taken over the centuries, thinking of all the futile deaths that would have to be endured before the Upright Ones could fully understand. Then, raising his weapon arm with the hand empty and open as a sign of greeting, he walked slowly towards the spears.

And as he walked, he tried to banish the personal fear from his heart and from his eyes, knowing that fear breeds fear; and, therefore, anger and violence. There was a smile on his lips; and at every two or three paces, he uttered a single word, hoping that intention and act would combine with sound to create the miracle of language.

As he approached the Upright Ones, the man who had laid down his spear lifted it once more. Again, there were three spears pointing at the man of the People.

But it was now too late to stop or turn back. So, repeating his word softly yet urgently, he continued on towards them.

The spears were neither thrown nor lowered. Almost hidden by three shaggy manes of hair, three pairs of bright, alert eyes regarded him with suspicion but without fear. For he was alone and unarmed.

And there would be many magnificent, misunderstood or futile gestures before the Upright Ones could ever hope to learn the meaning of the word *"Peace!"*

WHO NEEDS MEN?

EDMUND COOPER

Rura Alexandra, Madam Exterminator, had recently graduated into a 25th century world where men had become biologically less important, where women could reproduce as they wished by cloning and parthenogenesis.

Her task was simple – in theory, if not in practice; to wipe out the last few thousand men who had taken refuge in the Highlands of Scotland.

But an ambush near Loch Lomond led to rape, and the killing of her fellow-exterminators. And Diarmid MacDiarmid, the last remaining rebel chieftain proved too much of a fascination.

CORONET BOOKS